SEESAW MILLIONS

Cover design by Don Munson
Book design by Iris Bass

SEESAW MILLIONS

Janwillem van de Wetering, 1931–

AVAILABLE
PRESS

BALLANTINE BOOKS • NEW YORK

An Available Press Book

Copyright © 1988 by Janwillem van de Wetering

All rights reserved under International and Pan-American Copyright Conventions. Published in the United States of America by Ballantine Books, a division of Random House, Inc., New York, and simultaneously in Canda by Random House of Canada Limited, Toronto.

Library of Congress Catalog Card Number: 88-91976

ISBN 0-345-35693-4

Manufactured in the United States of America

10   9   8   7   6   5   4   3   2

CONTENTS

ROTTERDAM

CHAPTER 1

IN SINGLE file, a taxi, a not too recent Porsche, and a nondescript compact, entered a majestic apartment building's parking lot.

A tall, wide-shouldered, and blond-haired man emerged from the cab. His bow to the Porsche made his ponytail bob. "Hi Mark,"

"Hi, Syben," the Porsche owner said.

They spoke in low voices, intoning a secretive solemnity that seemed hardly necessary, since there was no one about except the cabdriver, who was on his way out, and the man getting out of his compact.

"Dad is dead," Syben said to his brother Mark.

"Yes," Mark said. He was about as tall as Syben. His unbuttoned overcoat displayed an elegant three-piece suit. His eyes, shielded by horn-rimmed spectacles, were hard to see, and his dark hair was disarranged by the breeze.

The third man's short legs were reaching for the pavement. He waved. This personage was definitely poorly dressed, in a windbreaker lined with imitation fur, patched trousers, and worn sandals. He was very small but had a large head partly hidden by a full, curly beard.

"Hi, Little Giant," Mark and Syben said.

Little Giant smiled at his brothers. He had just turned forty and was somewhat younger than Mark and much older than Syben. Little Giant shook Syben's hand first, perhaps because Syben made the most striking impression. The low sun's rays caused Syben's golden hair to glow. The breeze played with his majestic cape, turning its flaps into wings.

Angel Syben, Little Giant thought, is dispatched by heavenly authorities to check on the citizenry of Rotterdam, to make sure all is well with us. Little Giant often thought unusual thoughts. He was an artist, willing to acknowledge bizarre aspects in the ordinary. Little Giant made a living out of weaving baskets. His work, which he sold in modish stores, ventured occasionally into the abstract and into odd shapes.

"Dad is dead," Little Giant said.

"Yes," Mark said. "Why don't we go inside?"

Mark, followed by his brothers, strode up the stone stairs, pushed through the revolving door, and said to the doorman, "Sobryne."

The doorman knew that Mark was a Sobryne, and Mark knew that the doorman knew. Mark obeyed the rules of custom. A doorman's presence has to be acknowledged, for he forms a solid link in the useful chain of formalities.

"Please go right up," the doorman said.

The elevator carried up the silent brothers. Emerging on the top floor, they walked on the marble-lined corridor's thick carpet and gazed down at the lake, where slowly shifting colors, from deep purple to almost black, fit in with their thoughts of death—summer's death and their father's departure. Little Giant thought that his father's spirit might still be about, lingering near his beloved Mathilde but ready to get away as soon as his sons arrived.

Mathilde opened the door and stepped back, holding a handkerchief. Her lower lip trembled as she greeted her dead lover's sons. Well, lover . . . let's be reasonable: Old Mr. Sobryne was well into his seventies, and Mathilde had barely turned thirty. There would have been some relationship all the same; the couple had lived together for three years at least and shared a king-sized bed in the enormous bedroom in the rear of the apartment.

"Can we see Dad?" Mark asked.

"Certainly." Mathilde's voice was veiled. She had the voice of an elf (Little Giant had said that once), a water-elf whom you suddenly meet while vacationing on the water. The elf whispers secrets about you and about herself, supplies information that deepens your life, so that you suddenly know everything is quite different, really, and rather more beautiful than you suspected.

Little Giant sat down and waited for Mark's return from the bedroom and, in order to be busy, watched what was happening on the face of a tall standing clock. He found the various mechanical and rhythmical scenes irritating, so he looked away again and admired a collection of rare chinaware displayed in a rosewood cabinet.

Syben waited too, somewhat stooped, his slender hands clasped behind his back. The apartment's view was wide, and he thought he could see his father's soul flitting to ragged, silvery clouds on the horizon. Death is birth—a new being of quite a different order was leaving them now. Not death, but change, Syben's guru had explained a few years earlier in his profitable Himalayan ashram. The guru was an egocentric and short-tempered fellow who attracted young female disciples whom he liked to fondle while he lectured. Syben, who distracted the devotees' concentration, had been asked to leave after an apprenticeship most limited in time. He hadn't been able to learn much but now remembered shreds of the swami's doctrine. What was it again? No end? No beginning, either? Well, why not? Syben thought of circles meeting themselves at every point, and of lines elongated forever. So what is death?

Mark returned, and Little Giant took his place at the bedside of the corpse. He held his father's hand, remembering the old man's kindness, his continuous concern about his sons' welfare, and his willingness to pay bills, to listen, play games, and go for walks with him. That was still in the old house, Little Giant thought, that funny medieval building with the little towers poking out of the roof. You sold it when Mother died. Remember how you would take me fishing, and I could scoop up the carp with that long-handled net? And the Sunday mornings when you brought out the miniature zoo? All the little plaster of Paris animals, the cages, the fences? And your stamp collection, when I was old enough to sort out the doubles and slide them into your stock books? Those were good times.

"Syben?"

"Sure." Syben squatted next to the bed. His hand slid across the folded sheet until his fingertips touched those of his father. I am directed by half your chromosomes, Syben thought, so half of you is me, but yet we were never close. Not far away, either, though. Did my ideas frighten you a little? I always respected you. We looked alike, Syben thought, although I came out bigger. Same blue eyes, same high forehead; even our mouths are fairly similar.

"You're so neat," Syben whispered, almost in horror. Old Mr. Sobryne did look like a wax doll, in his pressed pajamas. Mathilde had shaved him well and combed his thin hair.

Thanks, Syben thought, for always writing to me for my birthday, if you happened to know in what country I was hanging out. I also appreciated your invitations here, after I came back, and your offer to buy me living quarters because you had paid for Mark's studies, you said, and bought Little Giant his cottage, and I never cost you much. I wish you wouldn't look like an envelope now, discarded after the letter has been read.

Syben didn't think about the inheritance, but Mark did. There will be a lot of money, Mark thought, which is good, because I've just been fired, and now I don't have to apply for humiliating unemployment payments. Dad saved me just in time. I shouldn't think that way, but I do. I also find Mathilde very attractive, and I'm excited by her sudden availability. It's a pity times have changed. Wasn't a dead father's concubine the oldest son's legal slave in old and better days?

His father's inheritance also occurred to Little Giant. He brushed the idea away. For the moment his memories were more pleasurable. Once, when he was a child, his father had handed him a group of toy animals, each wrapped up in tissue paper. He had to fold the paper away carefully before placing the animals in their cages.

Mathilde poured coffee; her thigh brushed against Little

Giant's knee. Why unwrap the past? Little Giant thought. What's wrong with the present? He watched Mathilde walk away to the sideboard and come back carrying a coffee cake on a tray. Can't I unwrap *her*? Unbutton Mathilde's tight black frock? If I do, it'll fall down gently. A tight but lush body, Little Giant thought, with supple rounded hips and a full, firm bosom, high above her narrow waist. Long legs. Can I weave all that out of cane? Out of reeds? My intentions are excellent; I'm an artist in need of a model. Mathilde is an ideal model.

My intentions are not excellent, Little Giant admitted.

Mark drank his coffee, ate his cake. He also watched Mathilde. One should never compare, Mark thought, for each being is unique, but I'll compare her, nevertheless, to my ex-wife, Geraldine. When I compare Mathilde to Geraldine, Geraldine is nowhere. It's hard for me to see her now. Mathilde has refined taste in clothes; Geraldine has none. Mathilde is tall; Geraldine is dumpy. Didn't Geraldine talk a lot? Isn't Mathilde a quiet woman? And yet, Geraldine had the guts to state—to my own friends, mind you—that whatever I would say at times would bore her to tears. How could I possibly be boring? What about my Ph.D. in economics, *cum laude*? Silly Geraldine. Perhaps she shouldn't have been so eager for a divorce. No kids—a pity perhaps, but not anymore. I'm alone. I didn't want to be alone, but now that I am, my share of the inheritance is mine alone. I don't want Dad to be dead, but he is. The king is dead; long live the king. I shouldn't be thinking this way, Mark thought, but I am.

"More coffee?" Mathilde asked.

"Please." Syben held up his cup. Aren't you a dish? Syben thought casually. For a moment he considered his father's wealth. This is a moment of abrupt change, Syben thought. I haven't got any idea about what will happen next, but I've lived through moments like this before—just before I entered the ashram, and shortly after I left. Several times in Chad, when I was fighting the bad guys. And again in South Africa, twenty feet underwater, with sharks coming for me.

Mark cleared his throat. "Mathilde?"

"Mark?"

"Would you happen to know if Dad left a will?"

The money, Syben thought, is about to descend. A rich man cannot, as I do now, live in a loft surrounded by junked machinery left by the previous occupant. Pity, isn't it? I rather like my loft. Will the sudden clang of gold disturb my peace? It undoubtedly will. What about my careful planning? I still have savings from the abalone fishing off the Cape Coast. I was going to ruminate for a while, read some books. Karma, Syben thought, that's what this is. My own karma, for me to adjust to. He cheered up. Sudden wealth can't be altogether bad, but it's a pity that Dad had to die for me to become wealthy, although it couldn't be otherwise, because he was getting old, and he was often ill. Change can't always be smooth; I must understand that.

"The will," Mathilde said, "is in the bedroom, and I will get it in a moment, but your father left a tape that I think we should hear first."

"A tape?" Little Giant asked.

"Containing your father's final message."

"A bodyless voice?" Little Giant asked. "While the body lies quite dead in the next room? That's horrible. Can't we listen to the tape later? Can't we have a drink first?"

"Yes," Syben said. "A drink." He watched Mathilde walk to the antique Flemish cupboard where his father kept his liquor. He heard Mathilde's frock rustle against her silk stockings and smelled her perfume. Her perfume suits her well, Syben thought; the fragrance is alluring, yet detached. Dad must have enjoyed Mathilde's company.

Mathilde had opened the heavy cupboard's thick oak doors. Crystal bottles, each with a silver label, sparkled. "What will it be?"

"Bah," Mark said.

"Nothing for you?"

"A cognac, please," Mark said. He turned to Little Giant. "I said 'bah' because I feel guilty. Dad kept those bottles especially for his guests. I've never thought of that until now.

For me, maybe. I always had to be pampered with Calvados, cognac, bourbon, Russian vodka. All he ever drank was good Dutch genever, from a jar out of the refrigerator. I wonder what he thought about my exquisite taste? You think he minded?"

"Not much," Little Giant said, stroking his beard.

"A true gentleman," Mark said. "Simple in his tastes." He laughed. "Remember his rhymes? 'Nifty thrift builds a house like a castle'?"

Mathilde laughed, too. " 'Builds a louse like a mouse.' He did change his rhymes, you know. That's what he made up for me. When I wanted to economize."

"Yes," Syben said. "I noticed that, too. Every time I came home from a trip, I found him more mellow. More rebellious against tradition, too, perhaps, or maybe I just wanted him to be."

"Perhaps it was the approach of death," Mark said.

"Lurking in the shrubbery behind the parking lot?" Mathilde asked. "Whenever we went out, he would point the place out to me. He wasn't frightened, though."

"What?" Little Giant asked.

"He knew he would die soon. Death was waiting for him."

"But he wasn't frightened," Syben said. "I'm glad."

"I won't have the cognac," Mark said. "Genever will do. I'll fetch the jar from the refrigerator." He came back and filled the three glasses Mathilde had put out. Little Giant fetched a fourth. "You, too, Mathilde. This is an occasion."

Mark raised his glass. "To Dad."

"Wah," Little Giant said. "Strong stuff. Death lurking in the shrubbery, hey? A skeleton partly covered by shredded skin leering from the greenery! I don't know whether I like that."

"I think your father did look forward to the end," Mathilde said. "He said he had made a lot of mistakes, and he was ready to face the consequences."

Syben refilled the glasses. "They weren't serious mistakes, but he did call *me* a louse once, when I left school and didn't want to study. He said I was wasting my genius, but later he seemed to change his mind. There were times when I thought that he approved of my wandering."

"I was a louse, too," Little Giant said. "When I went into art. Dad didn't believe in weaving reeds."

"I was never a louse," Mark said. "He liked me a lot."

"The tape?" Mathilde asked.

Mark shuddered. "One more drink, please."

The sun, ready to dip away, managed to break through the clouds. Strong light flooded across Syben. Little Giant gaped.

"I think you should have another drink, too," Syben said. "How did Dad die, Mathilde?" He picked up the genever jar.

"No more after that," Mathilde said. "I don't want you to be drunk when he speaks. Your father didn't feel well all week, but this morning he seemed to do better. He had breakfast in bed, and afterward he wanted me to bring in the recording gear and the tapes. When he finished speaking, he lay back against the pillow. He looked at the wallpaper and kept smiling. Apparently the lines on the paper moved for him, disappearing into the ceiling and coming back from the floor. He said the lines were illuminated and a lovely sight. Then he held my hands, dozed off, and died."

"The doctor?" Mark asked.

"Came too late. He left a signed statement that I put away with the will." Mathilde picked up the empty glasses and the jar. Her audience watched her slender fingers close around the porous phallic vessel.

"Ready?" Mathilde asked.

The brothers nodded.

Mathilde walked to the tape player, part of an electronic construction built into the wall paneling. A sigh emerged from the four loudspeakers placed in the room's corners.

"Boys, there you are, alive and well," the tape hissed softly. "And to you," old Mr. Sobryne said, "I direct myself, me, your departed dad."

CHAPTER 2

THE THREE men suddenly sat upright, and Mathilde began to tremble. Old Sobryne's voice was more realistic than the familiar intonation they all remembered. The startling effect of the voice, Mark reflected, wasn't only due to the equipment's good quality but was also probably caused by the unique situation. His father had often talked to him, and he hadn't sat up then, but during those occasions there were distractions. The conversations had never seemed important. Whatever old Sobryne had tried to express could be clarified by questions and answers. The dialogue, Mark thought, is now finished forever. Dad is speaking, if not from the grave, then, in any case, from the other side of a definite partition.

The loudspeakers hissed as old Sobryne paused and started again.

". . . your father"—he coughed—"and your lover.

"There you are, and I'm not with you, because I'm dead, and the idea is odd." He was talking more quickly now, conscious perhaps of the revolving tape and its need to be filled. "I never thought it would happen to me, against all experience and observation, because everyone dies; the final fact is unavoidable. Even very old men try to ignore death, because it doesn't fit their routine, but lately the indications became more obvious, and I have reluctantly prepared myself. With some gratitude, I should add, I may not always have used life's opportunities, but it would be childish to blame death for my mistakes."

The tape crackled softly.

"I did try to argue with death whenever I saw it lurking in the shadows outside, or waiting in the elevator, or when the cheeky fellow joined me at the breakfast table. Why wouldn't I reach ninety, like my brother Jan? Or a hundred, like Uncle Henry? The doctor didn't think I would live that long. He's an honest man and complimented me by telling the truth, for usually, he said, he avoids the subject because nobody can accept death, and most feel hurt or angry at the thought of finality. The doctor told me that I'm just about done, and I'm grateful to him as well.

"Mark," old Sobryne said, "Little Giant, Syben, Mathilde . . . dear Mathilde. I'm talking to all four of you. I've never had a daughter until Mathilde entered my life, and she taught me much about the female principle—more than my late wife was willing to share. She was shy, and our marriage wasn't harmonious. You may not know that, but it doesn't matter anymore. We should have divorced. It would have been better for both of us, but the mutual corset that kept us linked seemed too comfortably uncomfortable."

The tape rustled on. Sobryne coughed again. "Yes. Mathilde, my daughter, the term may fit somewhat but isn't quite true. A private matter, my sons. Perhaps she'll tell you about our relationship one day, although I don't see why she should. Now, to business.

"The inheritance," old Sobryne said, "is yours, of course. A quarter for each one. Mathilde should have an equal share. The will doesn't mention her, in order to avoid unnecessary taxes. The authorities—will the authorities ever be able to comprehend human relationships?—consider her as an outsider, and the government would rape her most horribly. I don't even want to attempt a calculation as to the percentage of the tax, so you will have to take care of the division. As the three of you are my children, the excise tax will be minimal, and you each will have to pay her after you collect. Mark?"

Mark became nervous. It was without cause, for his father only asked him to fetch pencil and paper.

"Are you ready? Then make a few notes, please. There's

money in the bank. I will give you the account number and the amount, and the name of the broker who is holding my shares. My bonds you can trace through the bank, again, and there's also some cash in my postal account. Insurance will pay for my funeral, and there's no mortgage on the apartment. I have no debts."

Mark wrote down names, numbers, and figures.

"When you add the values of the various sums, you have a total of my official possessions that you can pass on to the inspector, while staring the fellow straight in the eye. This sum represents my lifetime's savings. It should have been more, but taxes have stripped me without mercy. . . . I shouldn't complain . . ."

The tape hissed.

". . . although . . . No," Sobryne said, "I will not complain. Mark?"

"Yes," Mark said.

"Write this down as well. The number I will give you refers to my secret bank account in Switzerland."

Mark's pencil scratched on the paper.

"What the Swiss bankers hold," Sobryne said, "was left me by my father, who got it from his father, again." He cleared his throat. "I didn't take care of the capital too well; it did grow a little, but I was never able to beat inflation. I've always been a financial coward, and the money just sat there, like a pig in a pen. It should be fat enough now and ready for slaughter."

The loudspeakers hummed. Mark's pencil tip floated in air. The tape in the cassette revolved soundlessly. Little Giant had tucked up his legs and was caressing his beard. Syben observed the dying light outside drawing hazy lines on the foggy horizon, moving like those other lines on his father's bedroom wallpaper.

Mathilde's large green eyes stared from above her high cheekbones. She lowered her eyes when she noticed that Mark was watching her. She withdrew her legs, straightened her dress. She's posing, Mark thought, but naturally, like a well-trained model. Was she a professional fashion model perhaps? Did I see her in Geraldine's magazines? What is Mathilde waiting for? For a grand total? For the total of a fat mouse that'll jump from its hole any minute now, to be hypnotized by her cat's eyes, so that she can grab old mouse by the neck with those perfect nails at the tips of her dainty fingers? I wouldn't mind knowing the total, either, Mark thought. Dad told me once he was a millionaire, but how much more than a million did he have?

How much? Syben thought. How much is much? How far will my share take me? It seems that he wants us to waste the lot, but the more it is, the more trouble it will cause.

I'm entering a golden world, Little Giant thought, but so did King Midas, and he almost starved to death, for you can't eat the silly stuff. Little Giant's heart thumped in his small, wide chest. Up till now, Little Giant thought, I've lived a quiet life, but it seems that I've come to the end of my peace.

"All in all," old Mr. Sobryne said, "I'm leaving you two million, one million above and one million under the table. The million above is inclusive of the apartment, and I've undervalued its worth because real estate isn't easy to get rid of these days. Two million, a little more perhaps. Which is . . ."

Sobryne paused, not out of choice, but because Mark had turned off the tape recorder. The red eye of the amplifier died away. Mark sat down again. He reached for his glass with a shaky hand. Genever stained his waistcoat as the strong liquor burned his throat. "Shit," Mark said, "that's more than I thought, half a million each. . . ."

Little Giant slid from his seat and switched the recorder on again.

". . . much money," old Sobryne continued. Mark wanted to get up again, but Little Giant pushed him back.

"A lot of money," Sobryne said once more. "You can spend it on something. Half a million for all parties concerned. Not quite enough to retire on, but I don't suppose any of you are visualizing the possibilities of never having to work again."

The loudspeakers were quiet except for their hardly audible hum. Then there were tinkling sounds, footsteps on a parquet floor, the clinking of chinaware.

"What's going on?" Little Giant asked.

"I gave him a cup of coffee," Mathilde said.

Slurping sounds, more tinkling.

"There are no conditions," Sobryne said. "You can spend the inheritance in any way you care to, but I may be allowed to voice my desires and expect you to listen before you decide whether to ignore my requests. You know—I suppose I can say that now—that you (I'm only addressing my sons now) often reminded me of a nest full of baby birds. Ever-hungry little rascals, always looking at me with their beaks open. Whatever I fed you, it never seemed enough. But maybe I was a silly bird, too, for I never stopped saving, and I never bothered to fly anywhere."

Tinkling.

"And I hated the office, the work in the evenings, the files I took home to study during the weekends. . . ."

Clicking sounds. Slurping.

"When was this tape made?" Mark asked.

"Last week," Mathilde said, "in this very room."

"I'm not complaining," old Sobryne said. "I'm only stating facts; they're not all bad. Parents are supposed to care for their kids and prepare for their own retirement. I did manage to raise you and increased my safe feeling. I nurtured my investments, kept an eye on my Swiss account, and paid attention in general. I felt comforted by numbers and figures that weren't real because I never made use of them."

The hissing silence was terminated by a click. Mathilde had been waiting; she was standing next to the recorder. She reversed the cassette and closed its little hatch.

"It may go the same with you," old Sobryne said, "if you just stack the money somewhere—and I'm not saying that that wouldn't be proper procedure with safely invested savings and profitable capital. How would society's grand pro-

jects ever be financed if nobody was tucking pennies away?
Now where was I?"

Mathilde's voice prompted him. "If you stack the money
somewhere . . ."

"Right, thank you dear. Then there will be a repetition,
another safe feeling, but undeserved. I advise against it."

Hissing.

"Advise against what?" Mark asked.

"Against a repetition," his father answered the unheard
question. "That's why I have a proposal. I suggest that you
delegate Mark, as the older brother, a man with some sense,
some experience, somebody you can send on an errand, as
your representative, and ask him to change the entire inheritance into cash. I think you may trust him, yes, a prosperous
patrician like Mark."

"Thanks a lot," Mark said.

"Dad has departed, Mark," Little Giant said.

"Dad is dead," Syben said, and pointed at the wall. "His
corpse is in the bedroom, and the doctor signed the death
statement."

"Yes," Mark muttered.

"Trust Mark," Sobryne said. "Let him go to Switzerland. I
filled in a form that you'll find in one of the stamp albums
next to my bed. I propose that Mark collect the Swiss funds
in cash, and sell the shares and bonds and the apartment
here. Have the furniture auctioned—it should be worth
something—and sell the stamp collection."

"I want the stamp collection," Little Giant said.

"You'll have to pay for it," Mark said. "Three-quarters of
those pretty little stamps are ours."

"Don't be greedy," Little Giant said.

Syben held up his hand, for his father had continued
speaking. Mathilde wound the tape back a little.

"Or maybe Little Giant should have the stamps," old
Sobryne said. "He always helped me so nicely when he was
little."

Little Giant grinned triumphantly.

"But now," Sobryne said, "listen well, because this is my

idea. What if you gave a little party? You could do it here if the apartment is still available, or otherwise in one of your own homes. Be certain all the money is on view, because I want you to see it for what it is. I never saw it; all I know about my possessions is what my bookkeeping seemed to indicate. I only stared at figures."

"Cash isn't for real, either," Syben said.

"Cash isn't real, either, perhaps," his father said. "It's paper, printed, colored, complicated by pictures and figures and watermarks, with numbers in the corners. Money only has value when you've got to eat, or if you're ill, or if you have to bribe the turnkey, if you're stranded and your car's broken down. I trust those calamities do not apply to you. The money I'm leaving you is paper, and it's value is essentially different from the value of any cash that you have earned yourselves and that is keeping you alive. You are earning money, aren't you?"

Hissing.

"Syben?" old Sobryne asked.

"I've got money, Dad," Syben said, "the surplus of my abalone fishing wages. Sufficient to live on for another year."

"I don't know," Sobryne said, "Syben is my prodigal son, who returned, but then he didn't want the calf that I wanted to fetch from my stable. I didn't insist; I didn't want to insult him."

"Never," Syben said. "Don't exaggerate, Dad. I didn't need any money, so why should you give it to me?" He was interrupting his father, and Mathilde had to rewind the tape again.

". . . insult him. But now he'll get half a million that he can't refuse, and there's the same for Mark, and again for Little Giant, and for my dear Mathilde."

Hissing.

"*My?*" the old voice asked. "I still have trouble in doing away with possessive pronouns. I'm leaving you as naked as I was born, no, even worse than that; I can't even take my nakedness with me." The voice faltered.

Mark got up and pushed Mathilde softly aside. "May I?"

He manipulated the buttons. The voice spoke and faltered again. "I want to know whether he was snickering or sobbing," Mark said, "I do believe he was snickering."

"Sobbing," Little Giant said. Mark replayed the tape.

"Both," Syben said, "first sobbing, then snickering."

"The cash has to be on the table," Sobryne said, "visible, within reach of all of you. Have a party, play music. Drink alcoholic beverages. Enjoy yourselves without restraint. Play games. But do reflect a little. Will you spend the money, or do you prefer to apply it to some positive use?"

Hissing.

"Waste it?" Mark asked. "Why should we waste it?"

"Don't waste it," their father said. "Money is energy, stored energy, mine in part, and your grandfather's, and *his* father's, mainly. That money is, partly anyway, the Sobryne family's safe feeling, but I saw grandfather and father die. The respectable banker Sobryne cursed himself and his life's effort in his final moments. My father repeated the performance. His death experience was even worse; he groaned in desperation when he looked back on his past."

"The fear of death?" asked Mark.

"It wasn't so much the fear of death," his father said. "I think it was his realization of missed opportunities. I will die more quietly because I face the future with more confidence. I trust in you."

Hissing.

The sons listened intently.

"That's it?" Little Giant asked.

"Farewell," his father said. "That doesn't sound good unless you are planning a lengthy journey, but I can't think of anything better at the moment. Farewell, my sons. Farewell, Mathilde. You're even more lovable than you are beautiful. You took excellent care of me, and I thank you for your services. I had meant to buy you some rest in your life, but you returned my gift and added much of your own. Farewell."

Mathilde stood next to the machinery and didn't seem to notice that Syben had gotten up and switched off the recorder. She looked at the wall. "I hadn't heard the end of this tape before." Mathilde was crying a little.

"You're not alone," Syben said.

"I think I would prefer to be." She walked away from him.

Little Giant brought her a drink. She took a sip and replaced the glass. "Thank you." She blew her nose.

"Well?" Mark asked.

"Yes," Syben said, "as far as I'm concerned, you can be our delegate, if you want to be, that is, and have the time. You're busy, aren't you?"

"I could take a few days off," Mark said. "And you, Mathilde? Will you appoint me as your representative?"

Mathilde sat down on the couch and extinguished the cigarette that she had just lit. "Do you have to ask? The will doesn't mention me. Shouldn't you talk to your brothers in order to decide whether I have a right to your father's treasure?" She got up. "I'll leave the room for a moment."

"Why should you?" Syben asked.

"You agree," Mark asked, "that we should share with Mathilde? Equal parts for each?"

"Certainly."

"You realize that what the tape says is not legal and that only the actual will is to be considered by the authorities?"

"I'll fetch the will," Mathilde said.

Mark unfolded the document and glanced through its contents. "It only mentions us, the sons."

"I think Mathilde should have her quarter," Little Giant said.

"Right," Mark said, "and I'm your delegate?"

"You are," Little Giant said.

Syben waved lazily.

"We're only talking about two million," Mark said. "You might take the trouble to express your agreement verbally."

"Yes," Syben said, "but you know what Dad said. Money has no value if you don't need it for urgent requirements. Printed paper."

"Nonsense," Mark said.

"What your father said was nonsense?" Mathilde asked.

"Or not nonsense. Whatever you like. I'm an economist, not a philosopher." Mark wrote himself an authorization, in neat calligraphy, on a notepad that Mathilde had taken from his father's rolltop desk. His brothers signed it. Mark got up.

"Would you like some coffee?" Mathilde asked.

"No, thanks," Mark said, "I'll take care of the funeral, too. Selling the apartment will be the most difficult item on my list, but I know an efficient real estate agent. Does anyone want the furniture?"

His audience didn't respond.

"The clock? For Little Giant's cottage?"

"Too big," Little Giant said, "and too noisy."

The clock struck the hour in thundering tones. A built-in miniature carillon, slightly off key, tinkled a loud tune.

"You hear?" Little Giant asked. "It used to drive me crazy when I was a kid, and then the clock was three stories down from my bedroom. And look at all that stuff going on." On the clock's large face figurines cut out of tin plate were plying their trades. A farmer beat his cow, a fisherman repeatedly caught the same fish from a pond, a woodchopper swung his ax. "I don't want all those people in my house," Little Giant said.

"The Flemish cupboard?" Mark asked. "The china collection? Dad's antique desk? Old furniture brings good prices these days."

"Have it auctioned," Syben said.

"All right," Mark said. "Mathilde, could I have the key? I'll have to be able to get into the apartment, and maybe you won't be home."

Mathilde studied her nails.

"No?" Mark asked.

"Why don't you phone me, before eleven in the morning; then I'll make sure to be here whenever you come."

Good try, bad miss, Little Giant thought as he tried to catch Syben's eye. Syben stared out the window. It was dark outside. A faint half moon was surrounded by a hazy circle.

"Very well," Mark said, "I'll telephone in the morning.

Good-bye Syben, good-bye Little Giant. As soon as I have the cash together, I'll let you know."

"Don't forget the funeral," Syben said. "I would like to attend."

"That's true. See you soon."

"I'll walk you to the door," Mathilde said.

"Mark was in a hurry," she said when she came back.

Syben got up. "I'll go, too. Thank you for your hospitality."

Little Giant stood next to him. "We face a shaky future. With the promise of half a million each, Mark is already forgetting that his brothers would like to be at the funeral." He touched Syben's arm. "Perhaps you should have been the delegate."

Syben arranged his cape and shook his head so that his ponytail flipped over his shoulder. "Me? Maybe you would never have seen me again. Am I not the prodigal son, never to be trusted?" He hung his head to one side and produced some spittle that trickled out of his mouth. "I'm not right in the head."

"You're really dribbling," Little Giant said. "Don't be disgusting."

Mathilde stood in the corridor close to Syben, close enough to be touched. Syben's hand was coming up already, spread out, ready to caress her shoulder. Mathilde's wide green eyes lit up as she pursed her lips and stepped back. Syben's hand landed near the top button of his cape.

"Bye, Mathilde," Little Giant said. "Will you phone me when the funeral has been arranged? In case Mark forgets?"

"I will," Mathilde said, "and I'll phone you, too, Syben." She unlocked the door and watched the brothers walk away through the corridor. Little Giant's hairy head hardly reached Syben's waist. He had to trot to keep up.

Mathilde smiled and closed the door.

She was carrying glasses to the kitchen when the bell rang.

"I'm sorry," Mark said, "but I've never been in this situation before. I suppose you'd rather not spend the night with a corpse. Can I come in a minute? I want to phone the undertaker. I guess he'll want to collect Dad's body and keep it under refrigeration for a while."

"Go ahead."

Mark telephoned. Mathilde brought him coffee and washed the dishes. Mark read the business report. Stocks were down. Commodities were down. Foreign currencies were down. Some bonds were steady, except some that were not. Precious metals were down. Some analysts thought things might be better tomorrow.

Mark sighed.

He stayed until the undertakers arrived, two large, bald men, scowling sadly to show that they cared. They wrapped the slight corpse in sheets and placed it on a stretcher that seemed weightless in their big red hands. They nodded and took their leave.

Mark waited. Mathilde brought him his coat.

"You're okay?" he asked.

She nodded, pushed him out softly. "Bye, Mark."

CHAPTER 3

THE TREASURE, displayed on Mr. Sobryne's coffee table ten days later, seemed out of place. There was something shameful about twenty bundles of one hundred bills each, about the all-pervasive shine of brand-new oversize thousand-guilder notes. Even Mark, who had stacked the notes just now, was offended by the splash of loud green that contrasted with the spacious, toned-down setting of old Sobryne's luxurious living room; the thick carpets in off-white shades, clashed roughly with polished surfaces of antique furniture: a rosewood standing Frisian clock, a mahogany antique chest of drawers, a cherry-maple rolltop desk, and low leather chairs and couches.

"Here you are," Mark said. "It took time and trouble to get the loot together. A cool two million. There was more, but I had expenses." He smiled. "First-class fares, the very best food good hotels can offer." His smile widened. "I was entitled, of course. I did the work."

Little Giant, mesmerized by all that money within easy reach, managed to wrench his gaze away. "How much did you spend?"

Mark waved vaguely. "Maybe not so much."

Little Giant waved, too. "Let's see some receipts."

Mark was smiling again. "You will query your own brother's dealings for the good of all?"

Little Giant studied the carpet, then the ceiling. He shrugged. "Okay." He touched Mark's arm. "Thanks. A difficult job well done! Was it easy to shake the Swiss account?"

Mark, staring at the money, suddenly looked upset. He held on to his trembling lower jaw. "No. Swiss bankers are like gnomes in a magic forest. They appear to be friendly, but they're full of tricks." He dried his hands on his handkerchief. "And the bounder who bought the apartment was a frog, a slimy toad, a conger eel with a sting in his tail; I had to throw in the furniture, and he still made a counteroffer."

"You accepted?"

"Yes."

"How much?"

"What would it mean to you?" Mark said. "The bill of sale is in my pocket."

"Let's see," said Syben.

"No," said Mark, "you haven't got any sense, either. Who is the delegate in this conspiracy?"

Syben forcibly turned his head away from the cash. He looked about him. "So the apartment is no longer ours? Then we should thank your toady buyer, your conger eel, for the favor of allowing us to still have the use of it."

"He's taking over tomorrow," Mark said. "I made our presence here tonight a part of the deal, as I thought Dad would want us to play his game in familiar surroundings. And here's the two million, as stipulated by Dad."

"Good old Dad," Little Giant said. Little Giant was dressed poorly again, in a worn-out jersey stained with paint, and patched-up trousers. He got up, shook a double page out of a newspaper, and covered up the money. He sat down again and directed his gaze toward Mathilde's legs. Mathilde had crossed her legs attractively, and her skirt had crept up from her knees. "Even your legs are green," Little Giant said. "I dreamed about your legs last night, but then they were pink, like they are now."

"Is that so?" Mathilde didn't smile.

Mark pulled the newspaper away from the money. His voice squeaked. "Dad spoke the truth. All of us deal with money daily, but one never really sees the stuff. You keep a bit in your pocket and you write a few checks. You mess about with it, but you never behold her in her majestic glory."

"Is money female?" Syben asked.

"Certainly," Mark squeaked.

"Don't speak so strangely," Little Giant said. "Go on, say '*Achrwa, Achrwa*,' scratch out your throat."

"*Achrwa*," Mark said. His voice regained its normal tone. "I'm sorry. Yes, money is female, to me, anyway. It fills up an emptiness in my soul. I suppose it'll be male, from Mathilde's point of view."

"No," Mathilde said.

"It's female to you, too?" Mark asked. "I do trust you're joking."

"Sexless," Mathilde said.

Syben stretched. His crumpled shirt of Indian manufacture reached well below the seam of his linen jacket. He was lying on the couch with his feet on the arm rest. His bare feet had slipped out of his sandals, and he was watching his toes while he cracked their joints. His hand waved in the direction of the treasure. "It rather reminds me of playing Monopoly. If you happened to win, all the Mickey Mouse money was yours, but Dad would put it back into the carton and slip the carton back into the cupboard. It was all just another thought. Maybe that's what it is again, and Dad wanted to show us the folly of our ways."

"*Achrwa*," Mark said. "Do me a favor, Syben, and stop acting like a hippie. Don't you think you're too old to behave like a twitty twerp? Do try to make an effort. What Dad is displaying here will buy twenty brand new Porsches with all their options. Imagine them, lined up and quietly gleaming in the parking lot."

Syben closed his eyes. "I'm trying, but I haven't got enough space. The lot is full. Little Giant couldn't even squeeze his junker in just now."

"Can you think of one Porsche, parked on the elm-lined driveway of a castle? The castle is yours, too."

"I don't need a castle."

"Syben only owns a quarter of the loot," Little Giant said, "one-half million—that's too little for a castle."

"Whose side are you on?" Mark asked.

"I'll help you," Little Giant said. "Syben likes to travel.

Think of a trip, Syben, to a country beyond the farthest frontier."

"The journeys I'm fond of," Syben said, "aren't very pricey." He picked up a note. "One fourth-class ticket with a Messageries Maritimes steamer from Marseilles to the Fiji Isles."

"Don't spoil the game," Little Giant said.

Syben replaced the note. "As you wish. The boat that we used for abalone fishing near Cape Town costs about a hundred thousand. I quite liked her lines and wanted to have her myself. I'm now shaping five of them out of thin air and anchoring them next to each other. I'm standing on Blueberg Beach and admiring my five abalone boats parked behind the surf. The sun is shining down on their white cabins. Are you happy now?"

"What are you going to do with five abalone boats?" Little Giant asked.

"I wouldn't have the faintest idea," Syben said.

"Mathilde?" Mark asked.

"Clothes," Mathilde said. "They're always much more expensive than you think. And whatever goes with them doubles the price: a brooch, a scarf. And the ointments and the tubes and the bottles and the boxes, they always cost the earth, too. But this amount here is out of proportion. Why don't you put it back into the briefcase, Mark; I can't think that far ahead."

"Little Giant?" Mark asked.

"Money," Little Giant said, "only has value if traded for something else."

Mark's arm swept down across the money, "So trade it."

"What I'd really like to make," Little Giant said, "is the ideal female form, woven out of reeds on a bamboo frame. To do that well, you need a model, of a perfect woman." He looked at Mathilde. "How much per hour?"

"Nude?" Mathilde asked.

"If you'd be willing."

"I would not," Mathilde said, "But if I were willing to pose for you, it would be for free."

"We'll never get anywhere this way," Mark said. He jumped up and pointed with both hands at the piled-up money. "It isn't enough to retire on. But we could invest it as well as possible and add the profits to our normal income. Half a million at, say, fifteen percent is seventy-five thousand. Deduct taxes, and half remains. It still adds up to something and could be spent."

"If I were rich," Little Giant said, "I would like to go somewhere for a little while. To the faraway sun, not to the close-by sun, because that's where everyone goes. On a beach, in a hammock, with a cigar. Or on a camel, adrift in a golden landscape." Little Giant sat up, moving his torso to and fro.

"A tramp's life," Mark said. "Not my way at all. You can share your dream with Syben. To bum about without a goal, is that all you can think of?"

"Hold it," Syben said. "Let's try and stay polite, Mark."

"But am I not right? Isn't that what you are, a stylish tramp? You seem to be very good at it, but think of poor Little Giant, trying to imitate your elegant example. Can you imagine Little Giant as a knight in ragged armor?"

"Why not?" Syben asked.

"Sir Older Brother," Little Giant said, "can put his clever comments in the enamel pisspot that he used as a vehicle when he was little, riding it across the parquet floor. Maybe I don't look too stylish, but my clothes have been washed, and my small size is due to one of nature's many errors. I was meant to be a dainty elf but was born a human being by mistake. It doesn't mean that I haven't been able to take care of myself in a reasonable manner."

Mathilde got up. "There's no reason to put each other down. You're a dear man, Little Giant, and you're rich, too, like all of us now. Didn't your father intend this to be a party?"

"Yes," Mark said. "Liquor. I've earned several bottles of the best. I haven't had a drop in almost three weeks, never had the time. And I kept carrying hard cash around, another reason to stay sober."

"Well done," Syben said. "Well done, Mark. I do appreciate your efforts."

"Well done," Little Giant said, "I would never have been
able to pull it off myself."

"Yes," Mathilde said, "I thank you for your trouble, Mark.
What would you like to drink? There's a cold buffet in the
kitchen. Would you like to help me carry it in, Little Giant?
I had it sent in because I didn't want to mess up the kitchen
again. I just finished cleaning and scrubbing to make a good
impression on the buyer."

"Dear Mathilde," Mark said, "a charwoman with half a
million under the mattress. A cognac, if you please."

"Genever," Little Giant said. "We finished up Dad's jar, so
I brought my own and put it in the refrigerator."

"I'll finish the bourbon," Syben said.

They raised their glasses and wished each other health.
Mathilde drank sherry from an antique glass with the *S* of
Sobryne engraved into its crystal surface.

"To our wealth," Mark said.

"To Dad," Little Giant said.

"To craziness," Syben said, "because this is far beyond the
superior man's scope. I find the event hard to accept. Possessions are a heavy burden."

"Asshole," Mark said. "I do beg your pardon, Mathilde."

Mathilde carried in a tray. Little Giant brought in another.
Syben refilled the drinks. Mark observed the delicacies.
"Smoked eel and jelly, salmon on toast, Russian filled eggs,
crayfish salad, fresh shrimp. Cheese. No caviar. That's good.
We don't have to shovel the money out of the window."

Syben stood next to him. "There seems to be no limit to
the spread."

"We'll have to eat all of it," Mark said. "Leftovers will be
lost, since we won't be here tomorrow. Where are you going
to live, Mathilde?"

"Why don't you move in with me?" Little Giant said. "I
own a pretty cottage on a dike. You need a break. When you
enjoy the view of fertile fields and contented cows, your
mind can rest."

"No, no," Syben said. "My loft is spacious, and I could rig
up another hammock. Why don't you live the free life for a
while?"

"I can offer all the modern comforts," Mark said.

"Wouldn't Geraldine be rather upset?" Little Giant asked
while he rummaged through the cheese selection, "if you
introduced a dish like that into your sedate household?"

"Geraldine is gone," Mark said. "We're divorced."

"Really?" Syben asked, "I didn't know. You should keep
your close relatives informed of your calamities. Do you feel
better now?"

"You never liked her," Mark said, "and I don't think I did,
either. She has moved to Amsterdam and is living with a
girlfriend. She's working as a secretary to the Lesbian League."

Little Giant emptied his mouth, waving his arms to en-
courage his jaws. "I never knew, either. When did all that
happen?"

"Recently. I never thought that my ups and downs would
be of interest to you."

"You *are* my brother," Little Giant said, spearing some
salmon.

"I do appreciate all of your hospitality," Mathilde said,
"but I think I'm going to spend some time with my brother,
in St. Tropez."

"More liquor," Mark said, "and some music."

"Your father's favorite," Mathilde said, and switched on
the tape player. The music was delicate; slow-paced jazz,
with a muted trumpet and a helpful saxophone, a flowing
double bass and peaceful rhythm on drums.

"Women," Little Giant said, "we need more women. There's
an unfair division here, and Mathilde still really belongs to
Dad; if we would dare touch her, we would be guilty of
inappropriate forwardness." He spoke softly to Syben while
Mathilde danced with Mark, backing away whenever he
lurched forward.

"Some body," Syben said.

"Yes," Little Giant said. "You think, perhaps, that I know
nothing about women because I'm a dwarf, but you might be

mistaken. On my part of the dike most cottages belong to arty types, and I often have female visitors."

"You receive them successfully?"

Little Giant had gotten into the smoked eel and jelly.

"Any notable achievements?" Syben asked.

"Yes, especially since I learned how to go about it. It's a matter of waiting and reaching out when the other party drops her defenses."

"Would you care to explain?" Syben asked, sufficiently interested to look away from Mathilde for a moment.

"Women have a hard time," Little Giant said. "They are not appreciated by their partners, insulted, even abused. So they complain and select me as their comforter, because I'm such a friendly little chap, always ready with a cup of coffee, cookies, and"—he thumped his chest—"this here to lean against while crying."

"And then?"

"Then it happens sometimes," Little Giant said. "Often. Too often, really. Fatiguing, you know. I have to work hard for a living."

"So you're doing very well."

"But they're never as attractive as Mathilde. They would never inspire me to create the ultimate in reed weaving."

Both brothers were watching Mathilde, who was dancing alone as Mark twirled around her. His jacket had become unbuttoned and his tie undone. His hair was disheveled. Mark's movements adjusted to the bass's faster thumps and the more inventive drumming. The trumpet had broken through the limitations of the opening theme and was reaching for the sky, pushed up by the saxophone's hoarse tweeting.

Mathilde was still detached, in spite of all of Mark's efforts to engage her in his motions. Mathilde's black dress was made out of coarse lace. The openings in the material did not quite reveal her flesh because her shiny slip still blocked the view.

"Tantalizing," Syben said, "don't you think? What would Dad have done with her?"

Little Giant opened his genever jar, smelled its contents,

and recorked the container. "I do believe I would like something else now." He walked over to the cupboard, returned with a large glass, and poured from Syben's whiskey bottle. "Your very excellent health, brother."

"And yours," Syben said. "Do you think that Dad was still potent?"

"No," Little Giant said. "Mathilde functioned as his lady companion, and Dad was her gentleman friend. A mutual attempt to resist loneliness; a successful try, don't you agree?"

"When he was talking on the tape, Dad said he considered her to be his daughter."

"As a bit more, perhaps?" Little Giant asked.

"A most complicated relationship."

Little Giant swallowed two Russian half eggs whole.

"They must have done something together."

"What, for example?" Little Giant asked.

"I'm asking you," Syben said. "You know about women; you said so just now."

"Not as much as you do. I only know something about the underhand way. Mathilde is of another nature altogether."

Syben watched Little Giant through his glass. "What nature?"

Little Giant put his glass down and hid his hands in his beard. "I think," Little Giant said, "that Dad joined the erotic and the platonic elements and that he asked Mathilde, sometimes, when they were making contact, if she could, in this room . . ."

"Yes?" Syben asked.

"Walk up and down, in her stockings?"

Syben refilled his glass and looked at Mathilde. "Hmm. Yes. And her shoes."

"Just her shoes and her stockings."

"And her hair . . ."

". . . brushed down her naked shoulders?"

"Dad was a connoisseur," Syben said, "with a natural talent for subtlety. He knew what he wanted in his own modest way. He was a good example."

"But not quite perfected."

"Usable," Syben said, "but for me Dad never went far enough. I wonder if my attitude could be considered to be conceited. That worries me sometimes."

"But listen here," Little Giant said. "Just look at Mathilde. Let's face it; Dad did manage to get *her*, and he also did very well financially. I wouldn't even dare to think that I could equal Dad's feats."

"Right," Syben said. "A practical and gifted man. I like that. Admirable. A splendid example. But why was he alive? Why am I alive? Any purpose? Interesting questions, compelling, I think. Dad didn't think so. He just managed to march admirably straight ahead."

"An admirable man," Little Giant said. "I might imitate him, but I can't, and I don't have to. Dwarfs are exempt from all common rules."

"Dad wasn't all that tall, and you aren't that little." Syben held his hand flat, a little away from the table top. "Dwarfs are about this size. How tall are you exactly?"

"You mean with my shoes on?" Little Giant asked. "On tips of toes and full of air?"

"Yes," Syben said. "That's okay."

"Just under five feet."

"And Dad?" Syben asked.

"Five foot three." Little Giant's fist hit his palm. "And every inch a gentleman." He nodded furiously. "Even in pajamas. Even without. Last time I was here on a Sunday morning. Mathilde opened the door. I ran into Dad on his way from the shower, with nothing on. Even naked, he was elegant." Little Giant shook his large bearded head. "Perfect shape. Perfect gait. I walk differently. Dwarfs tend to wobble."

The music stopped, and Mark came to the table to pick up his glass. Mathilde arranged dishes, and Little Giant tried to help. His movements were unsteady. He attempted to fill Mathilde's glass. He steadied himself, leaning against the table piled with the money, which began to slip toward the edge. "I'll do it," Mathilde said. "You can turn the tape over."

"You have no idea of the trouble I had to go through,"

Mark said to Syben. "That Swiss banker was like a hysterical rodent defending the goodies he kept in his hole, and the bounder who bought the apartment seemed like a most unsavory crook. He kept sputtering in my face during the negotiations and leering horribly. And that damned money—I had to keep it in a safe, and every time I had to get at it there were creaking gates to be passed and identifications to be shown, and after all that, the containers would always be too small. I had to squeeze the money in and kick the drawers to make them shut properly."

Syben picked some of the bundles up that had slid to the floor and replaced them on the table. "It took you a bit of time, too. Could you stay away that long?

"I was fired awhile ago," Mark said.

"Here's to that," Syben said, raising his glass, "What happened? They didn't let you go because you took a week off, did they?"

"I was fired last month. The company I worked for was absorbed into another, and I became redundant. The bigger company is alive with Ph.Ds in economics." Mark took another drink.

"Did you mind?"

"Sure I did," Mark said, "and I minded the divorce, too. It isn't very nice to be not needed."

"You still had some dough?"

"No. The lawyers were nibbling, and Geraldine took what was left."

Syben patted the money on the table. "So this arrived just in time?"

"Yes."

The conversation, which Syben couldn't get away from because Mark's hand clawed at his sleeve, became more intimate. Mark talked about his marriage and other disappointments. He began to repeat himself. Syben listened, afloat on drunken, swirling waves that intermittently diminished and enlarged his insight into Mark's confidences.

"I'm getting a little nauseous," Syben said, "and there's still so much to eat."

"I prefer to drink," Mark said, "and because you're younger, you'll be joining me. Pick up your glass."

The evening moved steadily toward night. Little Giant was conversing with Mathilde, who didn't answer much, but kept the connection going by nodding and inserting a little question every now and then.

"Would you like some coffee?" Mathilde asked.

"Not yet," Mark said. "Why don't you have a little more sherry?" He was slurring his words; his eyes bulged in his round, wet face, and his spectacles dangled from one ear.

"No, thank you. Would you mind if I went to bed now?"

"Yes," Mark said. "You are a very beautiful woman, Mathilde, do you know that? It's a pity you have so many clothes on."

"Take some off," Syben said. Syben also had trouble with his pronunciation. He had to speak slowly; his mind had detached itself from the ever rising and sinking waves and floated high above, but he was still interested in what might involve him on lower, regular planes of existence, even if the spectacle made him sick. "I will take everything off," Mathilde said, "when I go to bed, but I'll be locking my door. You should stay over. There's a queen-size bed in the spare room; I made it up, and the couch is quite comfortable, too."

Little Giant reached for Mathilde's arm. "I'm already on the couch, why don't you join me, Mathilde? I know games."

"No games," Mathilde said.

"Didn't Dad suggest games?"

"Your father liked dominoes. This is not quite the moment. Stay where you are; I'll find some blankets and a pillow."

"Sleep well, Mathilde," Syben said. "No need to lock your door. I'll be looking in later to sit on your bed, tell you tales."

"No tales," Mathilde said.

"I'll be looking in, too," Mark said, "just looking."

"No looking," Mathilde said. "I'll like you all again tomorrow. Now you're in the way." She covered up Little Giant. Little Giant was asleep, bubbling sweetly far within his beard.

"A money-gnome," Mark said. "Endearing. Just look at that piled-up dough." He gestured widely. "What nonsense. All those zeroes."

"*You* shouldn't say that," Syben said. "*I* should say that."

Syben pulled Mark out of his chair and walked him to the spare room. He kept talking, referring to the wisdom of his bad-tempered guru, who, Syben supposed, while trying to get around a doorpost, might have understood something about something after all. Or was it that disciples understand, and then refer their understanding to the guru, who did understand once, or should have anyway?

A click signaled the end of taped music, another the locking of Mathilde's door.

Mark held forth simultaneously, impressed by his sudden insight into the meaning of money. Materialistic and idealistic theories were finding each other, Mark and Syben agreed, in miraculous and beautiful harmony. The defenders of opposing but no longer hostile faiths dropped jackets and shoes on either side of the bed, then shared the same sheets.

CHAPTER 4

"DID ANYBODY get at the money?" Mathilde asked the next morning. "It seems there was more of it last night." There was still money on the sitting room table: ten bundles of a hundred thousand guilder notes each. She pushed the bundles together while she cleared the remnants of the cold buffet.

"No," Mark said, and counted. "Yes."

Little Giant sat on the couch, washed and combed, holding his head. "What was that?"

"Half is gone," Syben said, counting with Mark. "You slept next to it. Did you touch the cash?"

"I was asleep, wasn't I?" Little Giant said, "and then I was given coffee, and then I was in the bathroom, with the two of you. So what is gone?"

"A million," Mark said. He sat down next to Little Giant and tried to open a package of cigarettes. His nails kept sliding on the smooth cellophane. Mathilde removed the packet from his trembling hand, stripped off the foil, and shook out a cigarette. She flicked her lighter.

"How did this happen?" Mark asked. "Who lifted the million? There were only the four of us in the apartment. The front door was locked, wasn't it?"

"Double-locked," Mathilde said, "and I have all the keys. Nobody could have come in or gone out."

"Through the fire escape, perhaps?" Syben asked.

"The fire escape can only be reached from the veranda, and the balcony door was locked as well."

"The windows?"

Mathilde got up to check. "All secured; nobody could have come in."

"So it was one of us," Little Giant said. "Who? Who is the despicable thief? Return the money at once."

He's making a joke, Syben thought; he doesn't quite believe it yet.

"Ridiculous," Mathilde said. "Who would like some more coffee?"

"Me," Little Giant said.

Mark's shaky finger pointed at Mathilde. "You're too calm. You did it. You hid it somewhere. You wanted to frighten us. Okay, you succeeded. You can give it back again now."

"Could I have that coffee?" Little Giant said. "And would you stop the quarreling? I can't stand shrill voices; that's why I live alone. And my head hurts, which makes it worse."

"My neck is sore," Syben said. "All that drinking wasn't a good idea, even if the idea was Dad's. Stealing money isn't a good idea, either."

Mathilde poured the coffee and passed the silver sugar pot and the milk jug. "I'm not too calm, but I didn't get drunk last night. I don't think anyone should lose his temper right now. I certainly won't, because you three inherited the money and allowed me to share. There's still some money, and I'm still sharing. I'm not angry, but I'm certainly surprised. Are you sure that somebody isn't trying to be funny?"

She looked at Mark.

"She means," Syben said, "that you should control yourself, too."

"Who is not controlling himself here?" Mark asked. "I only want to know what happened to the money. It has to come back to the table so that I can divide it into four equal parts. After that we can say good-bye to each other. Let's try and behave ourselves meanwhile."

Little Giant's hands clutched his beard. "Why don't you provide the example? Could you keep your voice down?"

"Who's the thief?" Mark asked.

Syben groaned and got up. "I'm the youngest son and often considered, certainly within the limits of my family, to be something of a ne'-er-do-well. Allow me to be the first to excuse myself. I never left the spare room until Mark woke me up this morning. I didn't take the money." He sank back into his chair.

"Right," Little Giant said. "My turn next. I spent the night in this room, but I was drunk out of my mind. The genever jar that I brought in was half-full, and I emptied it all by myself. I woke up when Mathilde gave me coffee."

"So you didn't steal the million?" Mark asked.

"Isn't that what I'm saying?"

"Not quite clearly enough."

"I did not steal the million," Little Giant said.

"Neither did I," Mark said, "and my innocence must be obvious to everyone concerned. I carried that money around with me for a week. Could I be trusted then and suddenly not trusted now?"

"Maybe you changed your mind but want to leave us some after all," Syben said. "You always liked grand gestures."

"Damn your—"

"No cursing, please," Mathilde said. "And I didn't take it, either. When I woke up, all of you were still asleep. That I'm still around proves my innocence, right?"

"We're all still around," Syben said.

Little Giant counted the remaining bundles. "There's still a million, and that's a sizable amount."

"We have to clear up the mess," Mathilde said. "The new owner will be here any moment. Won't you give me a hand?" She looked at Mark.

Mark nodded, held his head, nodded again. "Yes." He whispered hoarsely. "Right. We'd better clean up." He frowned at Little Giant. His voice gained strength. "But one of you is a thief. I suggest we stay together and move to my house at Juliana Street. I don't want any of you to slip away while this matter keeps us divided."

"What about dividing what is left now?" Little Giant asked.

"I will take care," Mark said, "of the remaining half, in everybody's interest. I'm still the delegate until further order.

Theft is illegal. Whoever runs away will be reported to the police."

Syben stood in the kitchen, a half-dried glass in his hand. Mark was washing up.

"Say, Mark," Syben said, "which million has disappeared, the million that's mentioned in the will, or the one that isn't?"

Mark soaped a dish.

Mathilde stacked plates. Little Giant scraped crayfish salad off the floor. "Did you hear what Syben asked?" Little Giant said.

"I did," Mark said, "and the question isn't new to me because it had occurred to me already. One million doesn't officially exist. None of us can prove that it was ever there, for the Swiss account carried a number, not a name."

"So?" Syben asked. Mark passed the plate to Syben.

"I don't know which million disappeared, but a quarter of it was mine, and nobody is going to walk all over me. You stay around, to avoid the deadly swish of the sword of justice."

"Don't threaten," Syben said.

Mark's dishwashing brush approached Syben's face. "You're not taking this lying down, are you?"

"Ah, well," Syben said, "as long as something is left, I won't get too excited. Anger is a disease, and revenge is for small minds only. I'm well above all that."

"He's well above all that," Mark said, "what about you, Little Giant?"

"I'm well below all that," Little Giant said. "And I don't want dishwashing soap in my beard. Take that brush away, Mark." Little Giant emptied the dustpan into the garbage pail. "But look here, Dad did leave us two million, not one million. I know I haven't stolen it, so one of you must be the guilty party. I would like to know how this will turn out, and I agree that in the meantime we should stick together."

"And you?" Mark asked Mathilde.

"Maybe you think I'm to blame," Mathilde said, "because I'm outside the family, and you don't know where your father found me. It's quite possible that I'm not too reliable, from your point of view. I know, however, that I didn't take the money. It's gone, and part of it is mine. I would prefer to stay together, too, so that I can see what will happen."

"I'm studying life in all its forms," Syben said, "and the present combination of material is interesting. It makes me take notice. I'll stay with you until the question is answered."

"Your highfaluting way of talking," Mark said, "is damned irritating." He broke a glass, "Goddamn . . ."

"Don't curse," Mathilde said.

CHAPTER 5

MARK was standing in front of the sitting room window. "It's raining," he said. "Yesterday it was raining, too. It'll rain again tomorrow."

Syben lay on Mark's couch. He was reading the collected works of Swami Vivekananda. Little Giant was walking through the room with his hands in his pockets. He kept himself straight up, as if he were bending backward.

"Don't trip over the edge of the carpet," Mark said.

Little Giant tripped over the edge of the carpet.

Mark shook a fist. "Goddamn . . ."

Mathilde came in. "I have to go and buy groceries," she said, "but I don't know what I should get. Nobody seems to like what I'm cooking."

"Your cooking is great," Mark said. "Every meal is a feast." Little Giant walked straight at him. Mark stepped aside. "Now that we're all together, I may be allowed to deliver a speech. Are you paying attention, Syben?"

"I'm reading about the inferior man," Syben said. "You remind me of the inferior man. I'm listening."

"Listen here," Mark said. "Fortunately we have been able to behave like adults during the last few days. The missing million has hardly been mentioned. But it appears as if it'll go on being missing."

Little Giant walked into the room at the back. He raised his voice as his distance from the others increased. "There's still a million left. Couldn't we do something with it? Hanging about here isn't getting us anywhere. I'm not saying that your house isn't comfortable, or that Mathilde isn't beautiful, or that it isn't a pleasure to be with my relatives, but even so, we *are* rich aren't we?"

"Are you proposing a holiday?" Mark asked. "I'm on vacation already, because I have been fired and divorced, and nobody is expecting me to do anything in particular."

"We are expecting you to do something," Syben said, "because you are our self-appointed delegate and in charge of our wealth."

"The wealth is in a savings account, growing slowly."

Silence returned to the room. The rain lashed the windows. A vacuum cleaner whined in the apartment below, the neighbors' baby screamed, seagulls clamored raucously in the gutter. The noise outside strengthened the silence inside.

"Let's go traveling," Mathilde said, "and look for a better climate."

"That'll hardly be productive," Mark said, "and certainly expensive, and it won't bring back the lost million."

"It's lost," Syben said, "and I don't see it coming back, but couldn't we make it somehow?"

"How?" Mark asked.

"There is a saying," Syben said, "that the devil always defecates on the biggest heap. I have been told, during my wandering, that once you have disposable capital, increasing it isn't difficult."

"How?"

"Commerce. Look for an article that is scarce and much in demand, buy it in quantity, and sell it at twice the cost. Double your capital."

Little Giant had wandered back into the room. "How simple."

Mark laughed.

"Don't be arrogant, Mark," Little Giant said. "An excellent suggestion. Syben is indeed a genius. Invest a million, collect two million, and the problem is solved."

"We'll be back at the beginning," Mark said.

"Yes," Mathilde said, and sat down on one of the straight dining chairs. "But can't we go traveling too? While we buy and sell? All this rain here is depressive and I'm depressed already. Do you know what you want to buy, Syben?"

"No," Syben said, "and my suggestion is perhaps too simple."

"Not in essence," Mark said, "and I only laughed just now because the truth of your hypothesis is so obvious. I was laughing at myself, really, because I should have come up with that solution. Haven't I helped to manage a company that specialized in that exact field? Buy for one guilder, sell for two."

"The company that was swallowed by another?" Little Giant asked.

"The net profit was too low because the cost was too high, but that factor doesn't apply in our case. Our cost is negligible, and we want to go on a vacation anyway. Let's select a country."

"Tunisia," Mathilde said.

"The article to buy?"

Mathilde smiled. "Hashish."

Mark sat down. "Hashish is illegal."

"Not in my way," Mathilde said. "Hashish is illegal here, but there's nothing against it in Tunisia."

"Hashish," Mark said morosely.

"Hashish," Mathilde said cheerfully.

She was sitting up straight and clasped her hands modestly. Mark saw her *en face*. Her face wasn't oval, as he had thought up to that moment, but rather angular, especially in the strong chin and near the eyes, where her cheekbones protruded sharply. Maybe I got used to considering her as a doll, Mark thought, but she does have a marked personality. The more I see of her, the more I admire her. I think she changed.

Syben saw her *en profil*. Mathilde's nose wasn't straight but slightly curved. He now knew that he preferred slightly curved noses to straight noses. Has her nose changed? Syben wondered.

Little Giant was looking at her softly rounded knees, and

her strongly rounded breasts. Fortunately neither her knees nor her bosom had changed, Little Giant thought.

"Hashish?" Mark asked. "Dope? Isn't that something for criminals? Our name is Sobryne."

"I'm aware of that," Mathilde said. "Your name is Sobryne, and you aren't criminals. My maiden name is De Gzell, and my grandfather was a Russian count. I'm not a criminal, either. That hash is illegal is due to stupidity. Alcohol used to be illegal in America, but that never stopped the business. Hash is available anywhere in the Netherlands. Did you ever smoke it?"

"I ate it," Mark said, "when visiting acquaintances. The hostess had baked it into the cake."

"Did you enjoy the experience?"

"Yes. It was a musical evening, and I never heard such beautiful music."

"But *was* it beautiful music?" Syben asked.

"Bach, played by an ensemble consisting of musicians employed by the ConcertGebouw Orchestra."

"Okay," Syben said.

"And you?" Mathilde asked Little Giant.

"I smoke it at times. As long as the experience lasts, the results are pleasant, but afterward I have to get up in the middle of the night to stuff myself on chocolate. I hate getting fat."

"And you?" Mathilde asked.

"Of course," Syben said, "there's nothing wrong with hashish. I wouldn't mind being stoned forever, but I do have other things to do."

"Shall I continue?" Mathilde asked.

"You have thought of a plan?" Mark said.

"I have a plan. My brother phoned the other day. He lives in St. Tropez, is most trustworthy, and imports hashish. The hashish originates in Tunisia, and he collected it himself until recently, but that isn't possible anymore. Does anyone have a map?"

Mark got an atlas.

"Here," Mathilde said. The Mediterranean. Here is St. Tropez, and down here is Tunisia. See?"

The atlas was on the dining table. Syben looked over Mathilde's shoulder. Mark and Little Giant stood at her side.

"Don't push," Mathilde said. "The distance from Bizerte in Tunisia to St. Tropez isn't much."

"But what stops your brother from going to Bizerte?" Syben asked.

"He became too well known."

"To the police?"

"The police are very helpful, but the competition wants to kill him. The importers are warring, and my brother's contacts aren't as strong as they used to be."

Little Giant's finger roamed over Tunisia. "Those yellow parts are desert. Do you think I could ride a camel?"

"Yes," Mathilde said, "but first you'll lie in a hammock and smoke some cigars. My brother wants us to take our time to get used to the country and suggests that we should spend a few weeks in a club on the beach. Clubs are very comfortable over there, and we could rent cabins overlooking the dunes. Meanwhile I can make contact with Achmed."

"I should be against this," Mark said, "but I'm all for it. If society pushes me out, I no longer feel subject to its rules and regulations. I also have pleasant memories due to the drug. Who is Achmed?"

"Achmed is a very nice man. Your father knew him, because your father and I stayed with my brother. Your father also wanted to ride a camel and smuggle dope, but Achmed had brought neither."

"Was that in St. Tropez or Tunisia?"

"We also stayed in Achmed's home in Tunis, but that'll be impossible now because Achmed and we shouldn't be seen together."

"A little travel couldn't do any harm," Mark said. "Don't you think so, Syben?"

"I've been traveling for years," Syben said.

"And we could invest a small amount first, and try again on a larger scale later. Until the million has returned."

"From here to *there*," Little Giant sang. "From *here* to there. And always on a camel, eh, Mathilde?"

"Yes, because we'll have to keep crossing the desert."

"But we do take a lot of risks," Mark said, "even apart from the money."

"We could limit ourselves to a quarter of a million," Mathilde said, "and say that it's *my* quarter. If the plan fails, I'm out, but if we succeed, my profit will be added to the capital, and the next one can have a try."

Syben was still studying the map. "But what, exactly, are we supposed to do?"

Mathilde indicated locations. "Here the hashish will be supplied, far into the hinterland, by Achmed's cousin, Saud, the Tuareg sheikh. Our next move is to transport the drug across the country to the coast, load it into a boat, and cross the sea. My brother will meet us in international waters in his speedboat. He will collect the cargo."

"And what could go wrong?"

"The competition could attack us, but why would they suspect us of carrying hashish? We will pretend to be archaeologists, drive in a truck, wear pith helmets, lug cameras, and carry spades."

"And who pays for all that nonsense?"

"Achmed," Mathilde said. "They pay for all expenses, and we collect the profit. That should be simple, shouldn't it?"

TUNISIA

CHAPTER 6

LITTLE Giant lay in a hammock stretched between two palm trees and smoked a cigar. Up till now everything is simple enough, Little Giant thought. I'm not simple, though, because I'm a dwarf, and dwarfs are freaks that have been put together in a most complicated manner. He watched Mathilde walking on the beach. Mathilde was dressed in a bikini. Sunset was close. Behind her broke long waves, set alight by the low sun's rays, across white egg-shaped polished rocks, randomly but artistically placed. Mark and Syben also relaxed in almost horizontally adjusted hinged beach chairs on the cabana's veranda. They were smoking cigars, too, and sipping sundowners. Mark and Syben were also watching Mathilde.

The club was exclusive, with no more than ten cabanas spread along half a mile of beach, protected against trespassers from the tourist hotels farther along by uniformed guards and dogs.

My body is very much like Syben's, Mark thought, but I've gone soft because of lack of exercise. I have a bit of a belly, and my skin is too white, but otherwise I'm still in fairly good shape. I've wasted too much time in dingy offices. The adventurous life will repair the damage.

"Well?" Mark asked, and pointed his cigar at the beach.

"Lovely," Syben said. "The picture is complete. Eternal and effortlessly moving green-blue water, pure white sand, smooth palm trees, decorative rocks, and a naked woman in between."

"She isn't naked."

"From this distance she might as well be," Syben said. "That bikini only consists of two stripes, shadows perhaps, thrown by palm leaves. Would Eve have looked like this? One might suppose that God, when he created the first woman, did his best, but that later, when the creative process had been initiated and degenerated into a routine, the attempt became flawed. A lot of women are kind of ugly nowadays, but the first must have been a goddess. Don't you agree?"

"Not really," Mark said, "but go ahead."

"The original woman," Syben said, "with the ideal figure. I would think so anyway, but tastes do differ. The way Mathilde looks conforms to the dreams of my youth. Long legs and narrow waist. Curved hips, high breasts, and a strong but delicate neck."

"The head?" Mark asked.

"I never really thought about heads then, but Mathilde's is most acceptable. I see nothing wrong with it. It has an inverted expression. And she's always polite, which makes her even more attractive. Where do you think Dad picked her up?"

"Under correct conditions," Mark said. "Dad wasn't the man to bother ladies. Perhaps there was a mishap in the street. She fell down and hurt herself, or her car malfunctioned. Dad invited her into his apartment—a cup of tea—and she never left."

"She was with him three years. Did she hang on because of Dad's money? Did she think he would marry her?"

"Mathilde doesn't appear to be a greedy woman," Mark said, "but the million got lost."

Syben got up. "I'm going for a swim. There are other suspects."

Mark held up two fingers. "You and Little Giant."

"Little Giant and you," Syben said, "because I know it wasn't me."

"Go on," Mark said, "we've been through that before. There are always three suspects, because the fourth accuses and isn't guilty himself."

Syben and Mathilde met each other on the path to the
cabana. He reached out for her, but she jumped away. She
sat down next to Mark.

"I was looking at you when you walked on the beach,"
Mark said. "You're beautiful. Annoying, really."

She looked at him through her lashes. "It's annoying to
have to keep listening to compliments. I know I'm attractive
to some males. Why harp on facts?"

"Why not?" Mark asked. "You're beautiful now, and beauty
is rare. Your shape keeps convincing me of your attraction
and causes violent desire. I keep wanting to go to bed with
you, and the excitement contained in the desire frustrates me
terribly."

"I don't want to go to bed with you."

"Are you sure, now? You're a normal woman, with necessities. You're wanted all the time. Doesn't that excite your
hormones?"

Mathilde lit a cigarette. "Oh, excuse me, that was your
packet."

"You're welcome," Mark said. "To bed, I said. Why not
now? Syben'll be away for a while, and Little Giant ate too
much. He's digesting in his hammock."

"No," Mathilde said.

"A pity. Lusty feelings plus opportunity give satisfaction."

"My necessities aren't your concern," Mathilde said. "I
dislike the expression anyway. I prefer 'expectations.' "

"Expectations . . ."

Mathilde blew smoke in his face but waved it away again.
"I don't have to discuss my expectations with you, either.
You forget the construction of our adventure. It's not just
you and me. We participate in a situation with your brothers.
If I become intimate with one of you, the balance is dis-
turbed, and the sympathetic basis of our relationship will be
destroyed. Then it'll be one of you and me against the others.
I don't want any outsiders."

"So let us take turns. Don't look at me that way," Mark
said, "I'm not saying that we should have an orgy. We'll

have you in turns, with the door locked, in total secrecy if you prefer."

It was quiet under the palm trees. The sea murmured and the wind rustled the bushes next to the balcony stair.

"Would you care for a drink?" Mathilde asked. "There is some fruit juice in my cabana refrigerator. I'll get it."

"There is fruit juice in our refrigerator, too, and Syben just bought a bottle of whiskey. In a minute. Let's finish this conversation first. What do you think of a respectable matriarchy? It's quite acceptable, especially in Tunisia. Behind us are the Atlas Mountains, and the Tuaregs live on the highlands. They're a proud and civilized race, and the men serve the women. My brothers and I would like to serve you, each in his own but efficient and modest manner."

Mathilde crossed her ankles. "Won't you stop your flirtation?"

Mark sat up and killed his cigar stub forcefully. "I'm not flirting. Flirtation is unserious courting. I've always been too shy for that sort of thing, too well-bred. I'm a gentleman from Rotterdam, and I speak the plain truth. I want to go to bed with you, but if you refuse, I won't be able to. I'll get the drinks. What would you like?"

"A weak whiskey."

Mark poured. "A weak whiskey, that's about a finger. Here you are. Want some water? Ice? I'll give you what you want."

Mathilde drank. "And I won't give you what you want."

"Is my proposal so distasteful, or ridiculous?"

"Mark," Mathilde said, "I don't want to insult you. Why should I formulate my private thoughts?" Her hand touched his wrist. "This is my adventure. I've got to concentrate; I want it to be successful."

Mark drank, too. "How is your adventure going?"

"I telephoned Achmed," Mathilde said. "It seems that his position has weakened further, and he doesn't dare trust anyone except his cousin Saud, who is far away. Achmed will park a truck in front of this club in a few days' time and send us the key and a map through the mail. He also told me where to rent a yacht. It'll need to be a fairly large vessel, because a quarter of a million will buy a lot of hashish."

"As far as I'm concerned, we can go," Mark said. "I bought the clothes and the camera. The spades and pickaxes are under the bed, and when Little Giant puts on his little round glasses, he will change promptly into Professor Sobrinsky, chief of the archaeological expedition in search of Christian scrolls in buried Moslem jars. I am the financial backer, and Syben will be navigating us across the wasteland. But I keep thinking that the whole thing is too easy. Your brother is a most charming fellow, and the hospitality in his villa was impeccable, but do you really believe that if we . . ."

". . . meet him on the Mediterranean and hand over the merchandise, he'll pay us promptly? Don't worry, Mark; we'll be supplying Paul with much-desired goods, most excellent hashish from the Tunisian highlands. He'll be most willing to pay and will have the cash ready."

"Whatever you say," Mark said. "It's your money. We're only going along because we happen to be around."

Mathilde's fingers clutched the cloth of her chair. "I wish it was your business, and that I was going along with you. Wouldn't that be delightful? Vacationing on a beach, a trip through mountain and desert? To loll about without a thought in my head?"

"Little Giant has been looking forward to the trip."

"Yes," Mathilde said, "But he might not enjoy himself so much once we get into it. Achmed sounds very worried."

"The more he worries, the better he'll take care of us."

"You do have the money, don't you?" Mathilde asked.

"Yes."

"Where?"

"Hidden."

"As long as you can find it."

"I can find it," Mark said. "But you can't, I don't trust anyone anymore."

"It's my money; you can tell me where it is."

"Nobody is not somebody," Mark said. "Hello, Little Giant."

"Come for a walk," Little Giant said to Mathilde. "It'll be

dark in a few minutes, and then it will be too late. I want to show you something."

"I've been for a walk."

"It's close by."

Syben stood behind Little Giant. "Be careful. Stay here. I'll have a drink, too."

"In a minute," Little Giant said. "We'll be right back."

Mathilde was wearing beach shoes with thick soles. Little Giant walked on bare feet. The woman towered above the little man. The little man trotted.

Mathilde scratched her back. "What do you want to show me? It's still quite warm, isn't it? The sand is tickling me, or maybe it's sea salt drying on my skin. I need a shower."

"Just what I thought," Little Giant said, "I've been swimming, too, and my skin is itchy as well. The showers are no good. Too little pressure. I found something much better. Here, behind these bushes. A shallow swimming pool for little kids, where they can play safely, but there aren't any little kids in the place right now, and the pool is dry."

Little Giant showed Mathilde a round basin lined with tiles. A rubber hose lay on the pool floor. "I just tried the hose and it works very well. The water is fresh. Stand over there, and I'll hose you down."

Mathilde stepped into the pool.

"Walk along to the other end," Little Giant said. "The spurt will easily reach you there. And don't feel shy; all the guests are in their cabanas, and the servants are having dinner."

He unscrewed the nozzle and aimed the foaming spray at her feet. "Ready?"

Mathilde raised her arms. "Yes."

Little Giant wagged the hose. Mathilde was still sandy.

"Go on," Mathilde said.

"Take your bikini off," Little Giant shouted. "Under the cloth is where it really itches."

Mathilde walked toward him with long strides. She looked angry. Her left arm dangled at her side; her right arm veered upward. Little Giant's foaming solid spurt pushed her back.

"No," Mathilde shouted. The water splashed into her mouth, hit her between her breasts, lowered to her navel.

"Off with it," Little Giant roared.

Mathilde stepped out of the bikini bottom and unclasped her halter.

Little Giant went all out. The spray touched Mathilde wherever Little Giant wanted, with force. Mathilde subjected herself to the treatment, humbly receptive. Little Giant handled the hose well, without spraying the spots of his choice too long.

"Turn around," Little Giant roared. The stream touched Mathilde's neck, followed her spine, richocheted off her buttocks, swept down her thighs, reached her ankles, and came up again. "Enough?" Little Giant shouted.

"Not quite," yelled Mathilde.

Mathilde wrung out her bikini while Little Giant rolled up the hose. Mathilde stepped back into her panties, resting one hand on Little Giant's shoulder.

"Shall I fasten the halter?" Little Giant asked politely.

"I think I can do that myself."

"You liked that, didn't you?"

"For shame," Mathilde said. "You were raping me just now."

"But you did like it, didn't you?"

"Yes," Mathilde said, "that was quite pleasurable."

"I only wanted to get rid of your itching. Otherwise, you might have come out with a heat rash. Most ungainly. I've seen it on the skin of some of the other guests."

Mathilde walked back to the cabana. Little Giant climbed the steps to the veranda, where his brothers were waiting for him. "Soon," Mark said, "you'll be on a camel. And now I will pour you a drink. Are you happy now?"

Little Giant said he was.

CHAPTER 7

THE grayish-green six-wheeled truck hobbled along a narrow winding road. The cabin was large enough for all four of them. Mark drove. "Are we going in the right direction? All these roads look similar."

"That man just now," Syben said, "who spoke reasonably good French, said we were."

"I do not speak reasonably good French," Little Giant said. "What else did the man say?"

"That Tunisia becomes beautiful once you're outside the city and that Tunis and the surrounding area are a horrible mess. He comes from the mountains, but there's no money out there. There isn't much in the city, either, because poverty is all over the place. He used to work in Paris, but his permit wasn't renewed."

The truck sloshed through mud. Little Giant tried not to look into the ravine, where gnarled little trees grew, olive trees, according to Syben.

"You're driving too fast," Little Giant said.

At the next curve the road ascended steeply. Mark geared down and turned the wheel. "I'm supposed to drive fast," Mark said, "the faster the better, so the wheels will grip the road. You wouldn't want us to get stuck, would you?"

"Isn't that wheat growing down there?" Mathilde asked. "That would mean they have some bread."

The grain fields came to an end. The road wound on, and the truck kept slipping. Little Giant looked down on new ravines and fields where black sheep and spotted goats gnawed at weeds. There were people, too, stooped and wrapped up in frayed cloth, who would cross suddenly, so that Mark only evaded them with difficulty, or raggedly clad children, who looked at them as they went past.

The truck hit a pothole.

The road narrowed and penetrated a village, protected by crumbling stone walls, strengthened at the corners with stump towers, leering suspiciously through slits designed for archers and handlers of blunderbusses.

Mark parked on the square, between a herd of donkeys tied together and a yellow bus decorated with bleeding roses.

Little Giant put on his plastic pith helmet and tried to clean the glass of his little round spectacles with his scarf. He was approached by men dressed in worn-out European suits, who hesitantly held up clay pipes and tough-looking brown cakes.

"That's good," Syben said. "They don't think we're hash buyers, but they're trying anyway."

Mark held Mathilde's arm as she stepped out of the truck. "Mathilde?" Mark asked. "Why do we have to go so far to buy hashish? Everywhere I stop, these gentlemen freely offer the product."

Mathilde looked at the gentlemen.

"I think," Syben said, "that the hash is still too expensive here. And the quality won't be good, either. It's probably *kef*."

And what is kef?" Mark asked.

"Marijuana, chopped, not purified. It'll make you high, but not very high."

"Twigs and all," Little Giant said, "and tobacco added for taste."

"What we're looking for is *zero zero*," Syben said, "the best of the best, and a truckload of it, if you please; that's not what they're selling here."

Mark pulled a traveling bag out of the cabin. "I'm only an uneducated tourist, and we're out of cheese sandwiches. Now if Professor Sobrinsky would take care of lunch, I will check if the gasoline here is the same terrible quality as in the previous village."

"Professor Sobrinsky, world famous archaeologist, has just discovered an atelier," Syben said, "where baskets are woven out of weeds. He shouldn't be disturbed. I will look for food."

Little Giant had squatted down between a woman and a boy who were showing him how to set up a basket frame. Mathilde smiled as she watched the small figure. She stood in the full light of the square. The hash gentlemen, perched on a weathered wooden bench, eyed her hungrily. A young man, dressed in a frock spattered with paint, seized her hand. *"Venez, s'il vous plaît. J'ai besoin de vous pour quelques instants seulement."*

"Mark?"

"I'll go with you," Mark said. "He says he only needs you for a few minutes."

The young man pulled Mathilde into a shed and pointed at some pots filled with paint. *"Attention, madame."*

"Mind the paint," Mark said.

"I know what he is saying," Mathilde said. "My French is better than his because I went to a private school in Switzerland, but what does he want of me?"

Mark sat down on a stool. "Isn't that clear? This artist paints paintings that he sells to the transport business. Didn't you see that all buses and trucks here are decorated? He needs you as a model."

"So why should I be his model?"

"Because you're beautiful," Mark said. "That means you owe him. I explained the principle to you before."

The young man grunted happily. A panel made out of silver-gray boards has been set up. The panel showed a blue field framed by twisted olive branches. The field was still empty but for a small cloud in the lower right corner. The young man touched Mathilde's shoulders with his fingertips and pushed her carefully toward the door.

"Mark?"

"You have to pose on the threshhold," Mark said.

The young man's fingertips slid down Mathilde's arms.

"Your apparel is exotic," Mark said. "You're looking heavenly in those narrow trousers, those high boots, that red sash around your waist. In his eyes you're a houri from the Islamic hereafter."

The artist put Mathilde's arms up, until her hands reached the doorposts. He folded her hands around the wood, pushed her chin to the side, and held his hand under her thigh.

"Mark?"

"I'm here," Mark said. "Nothing can happen to you. He wants you to raise your leg."

The young man turned Mathilde's torso.

"Mark?"

"No, it's all right. Now your bosom is properly outlined against the blue of the sky."

The artist dived into the shed's recesses, pushed a brush into black paint, and drew Mathilde's body on the panel.

"How long does he want me to stand like this?"

"I don't know. You're supposed to look appealing. You're a houri, you see, and you're entering the space, where the observer finds himself, in an inviting manner. Soon you'll be on the back of a truck and filling the fantasy of a driver who is following that truck, for hours maybe, because it isn't easy to pass on Tunisia's narrow roads. If you look uptight, you'll turn the fellow off."

"What's a houri? A whore?"

"A heavenly whore," Mark said. "The man who owns the beach club in Bizerte explained it to me. Moslems who live according to the rules will go to heaven, whither the houris await them."

Mathilde observed the painter's frantic efforts. "He's making my breasts too large and my thighs too fat."

"You think so?" Mark asked.

"Don't you think so?"

"I think you're the most beautiful woman I've ever seen, and so apparently does our artist. Just listen to his labored breathing. But I suppose everybody appreciates your attractions in a different way."

"He's making me plump."

Syben appeared. "We've got food and gas coming."

"The artistic liberty," Mark said. *"Vous permettez, monsieur, il faut partir."*

"Merci," the young man said.

"I detest goat's milk," Little Giant said. "What's in the paper bag?"

"Wheat cakes," Syben said. "They taste terrible."

"Medjez el Bab," a helpful hash gentlemen said.

"El what?" asked Mark.

"Bab," Mathilde said. "Must be the name of the village."

"Oui," the hash gentleman said, and pointed up, "Djebel Mrhila."

"The mountain?"

"Oui, monsieur, four thousand two hundred feet high. The devil lives up there, the *djebel.* Pay attention when you drive away from here because the road will be getting worse. Won't you buy some hashish from me? When you smoke, fear will leave you, and your driving will improve."

"He's driving badly enough as it is," Little Giant said.

Mark was distracted by a goat jumping across the road, and the truck slid in mud. He changed gears too late, and the engine stalled. A mountaintop towering baldly above the bleak landscape dominated the empty environment. Black dots circled high in the hot expanse of the sky.

"Vultures," Little Giant said, "waiting until we crash down somewhere. Then they'll flop down quickly, pull us out through the windows, and tear us to pieces."

"Without the engine noise," Syben said, "it's beautifully quiet here."

Mark reached out for the ignition.

"Whoa," Little Giant said, "I've got to go and visit a tree."

The brothers, standing in a row, urinated into a ravine.

"Man isn't much," Syben said. "Look at the result of our total effort. Three piddly rays of meager foam losing themselves in immeasurable space."

"I've got to visit a tree, too," Mathilde said, "but there aren't any."

"Try the bush over there," Little Giant said.

"I did, but there's something alive between the stalks."

Little Giant hit the bush with a stick. A yellow snake with red lines across its flat head slithered away.

"See? Maybe there are more like him."

Little Giant walked through the bush. "They've all gone."

"They'll come back."

"Do what you have to do," Little Giant said. "I'll be around. If anything dares to interfere with you, I will smash it to smithereens."

Syben and Mark walked away. "Teacher's pet," Mark said. "I don't like that at all. It spoils our relationship. When she selects Little Giant for support in troublesome circumstances, a group will form within the group, and we'll be out of balance."

Little Giant and Mathilde came back.

"How far from here?"

"Far," Mark said. "I don't understand the map too well. I believe there are more mountains ahead, and then the desert, and then another range."

Syben held on to the dashboard when they cut through the next curve. Donkeys approached, staggering under loads of bundled twigs. There wasn't much space left. Mark drove on without diminishing his speed. One of the truck's wheels spun over the precipice.

"You're driving too fast," Little Giant said. "You're show-ing off. I want to drive."

Mark drove faster. Mathilde covered her eyes with her hand.

The next village consisted of windowless square houses, their rotting doors hanging crazily between the flaking stucco walls.

One of the buildings was a restaurant with a courtyard. Geraniums in rusty cans had been haphazardly placed on sagging tables. A toothless woman brought brown porridge in cracked bowls and oversweet, thick coffee in earless mugs. She also filled the flasks that Syben held up for her, with murky water trickling from a goatskin bag.

Mark showed her the map, but she shook her head. "*Un moment.*" She came back, guiding an old man by the hand.

"My daughter can't read maps," the old man said, "and I don't see well, but you're not far from your goal."

"Do you know where we're going?" Mark asked.

"I have been told, *monsieur*. Saud sends his greetings and wants you to know that from here on the tracks will be bad."

The woman pushed her father gently out of the courtyard.

"Even worse?" Little Giant asked. "But this is a true adventure, isn't it?"

"Let me drive," Syben said. Mark was already behind the wheel.

"Never. You must allow me to be useful."

"By feeding us to the vultures?" Little Giant asked. "You keep driving too fast."

"I took a course," Mark said, "in dangerous driving. I passed, and I don't want to waste the money I paid."

The truck scraped past rocky walls and ravines; it stripped the bark off trees, rustled bushes, and narrowly missed goats and a camel. The camel was ridden by a man listening to a transistor radio pressed against his ear. The animal jumped aside, and the man dropped his radio.

"You won't be popular with the locals," Syben said.

Mark put his foot down. Syben fell back against the seat. A cadaverous pig stood in the middle of the road. "Whoa," Little Giant shouted.

"Mustn't exaggerate," Mark said. "You're a bad driver yourself. That wreck you own at home is always covered with chicken feathers."

The road straightened out. Syben pulled the key out of the ignition.

"Now what?" Mark asked. "We were making good time."

Little Giant dropped out of the cabin, staggered away, and embraced a tree.

Mathilde leaned against a rock. She spoke softly while looking ahead. "I have prayed. I haven't prayed in years, but it didn't work at all. I stayed scared."

"Nonsense," Mark said, "I was driving very well. With a heavy truck like this, one just has to keep going, or there's no fun in the game. Don't you think so, Syben?"

"I don't think so," Syben said, "and I'll be driving the rest of the way—as far as the desert; we'll see what happens then. This thing will never make it through the sand. That must be the desert down there. The Sahara may be the greatest stretch of sand on earth and one of the planet's miracles, but it doesn't mean anything to me now because I have stomach cramps."

Mark walked away.

Syben climbed behind the wheel and rolled the window down. "Coming?"

Mark got in silently.

At the end of the road a group of camels was waiting, accompanied by a tall, slender man holding a rifle.

"Saud," the man said, and pointed at his chest. Only glittering eyes were visible through the slit in his headgear. He unwrapped a cloth that he pulled from under the saddle of one of his camels and handed it to Mathilde.

"I think you have to wrap that around your head," Syben said, "as a protection against the sand and so as not to seduce the men around you. Tuaregs are very proper."

"This dirty rag? It stinks of goat."

Saud's eyes flashed.

"Wrap it around your head. Tuaregs aren't only proper, they're also short-tempered. If you don't do as they say, they'll be throwing rocks."

Saud tied the travel bag that Little Giant gave him to the camel saddle. He spoke to another camel. The camel knelt down.

"You'll have to mount it," Syben said to Mathilde.

The camel's bony knees cracked, and its tail swished as it clambered up again. Its eyes squinted above its grinding jaws.

The next camel was Little Giant's.

"Why do I get the biggest of them all?" Little Giant asked. "Aren't there any dwarf camels?"

"Hop," Syben said. "Your turn, Mark."

"You go to hell," Mark said. "I'll select my own camel."

Little Giant's camel wasn't only the biggest but also the

worst-tempered of the lot. It tried to push Saud's camel aside, but Saud hit the intruder with the butt of his rifle. Little Giant's camel snorted. "Hey," Little Giant said. "Help! I can't hold on to this thing. I'll slip off."

Saud pointed at Little Giant's shoes and at his own bare feet.

"You'll have to take off your shoes, tie them together, and hang them around your neck," Syben said, "just like I did. Press your feet against the animal's neck."

"I can't reach that far," Little Giant said.

"If you really want something," Syben said, "It'll come your way. You wanted to ride a camel. Enjoy the fulfillment of your wish."

The camels, mumbling irritably, chose their positions.

"*Oui?*" Saud asked.

"We're ready," Syben said.

"*Hùt hùt hùt,*" Saud said.

The column moved, the sand crackled. The evening faded, but the heat still scorched.

The desert slipped away under the camels' soft feet. Night fell, and a sickle moon painted the desert silver.

Little Giant moaned.

Syben turned, "Yes?"

"The ship of the desert," Little Giant said. "I'm seasick. Ask Saud if we can stop."

Syben pushed his feet into the camel's hairy neck. The camel trotted. "Saud?"

"*Plus tard,*" Saud said.

"You'll have to wait awhile," Syben called.

"Quite," Little Giant said, "but I have to throw up *now*."

"You messed up that poor animal," Syben said when they got off hours later and Saud passed his water bottle around.

Mark had walked away. Mathilde was stretched out on the sand.

"How are you doing?" Syben asked.

"Not very well."

"Saud wants to go on. Shall I say that we have to rest?"

"No, I'll manage. How do you feel?"

I feel very well, Syben thought, a little later, cradled by his camel again. This is as pleasant as sitting on the abalone boat, going out or coming back; it never mattered. Just moving to nowhere in particular, to be engaged without a goal, as I used to be in the streetcar on my way to school, or going home. It didn't matter then, either.

Saud slipped his rifle over his head, aimed the weapon at the sky, and fired. Another shot answered from a nearby hill.

A horseman, waving and shouting, galloped toward the caravan. His impatient horse whinnied and reared as he pulled up next to Saud.

I'm not angry anymore, Mark thought, astride the last camel, and I'm sorry that I don't drive a truck very well, but I've been punished sufficiently by now, and if I'm ever allowed to get off this badly assembled monstrosity, I will lie down on the ground and never get up again.

Small dwellings, built out of pieces of rock and covered by stone tiles, leaned against each other behind the hill. The camels knelt down without waiting for a command, and the travelers slid down to the sand. Mark lay where he fell. Little Giant staggered to the camel carrying the luggage and pulled out a flask. He drank, gurgled, and spat.

"Easy now," Syben said. "I don't think they have city water here." He unscrewed another flask for Mathilde. Mathilde walked over to Mark, lifted his head, and supported it with her knee. She pushed the flask between Mark's cracked lips.

An Arab took Syben by the arm and walked to one of the huts. He laughed. *"Le petit déjeuner?"*

"Thank you," Syben said. He walked back to Mark. "Get up. Food."

Little Giant trotted next to Syben. "Really? I'm hungry."

Syben smiled. "I'm pleased to hear it. How did you like the trip? I thought you were somewhat unwell on the way."

Saud stood next to Little Giant and pulled his sleeve. Behind them Little Giant's camel stamped its feet and swung its head. Yellow foam dripped from the animal's open mouth. Its tail hit its sides ferociously.

"Bad-tempered bastard," Little Giant said. "What does that man want of me, Syben?"

Saud grabbed Little Giant's jacket and stripped it off.

"I think he wants you to undress," Syben said. "Do as he says. Homosexuality is quite accepted among Arabs. You don't have to feel ashamed."

Little Giant attempted to defend himself, but another Arab picked him up and pulled off his trousers. Saud spread the jacket and the trousers in front of the camel.

"My expensive suit," Little Giant shouted, but it was too late. The camel, snorting and bleating, stamped on the clothes. Then it spread its legs.

"No," Little Giant shouted.

"He's getting rid of his anger," Syben said. "The camel thinks that you are the clothes because they smell of you. He is murdering you symbolically and humiliating you afterward. An outstanding example of applied psychology. If the guru had done that to me in the ashram, I might be a holy man now."

"That suit was brand-new, and now he's pissed all over it."

"But you're still alive," Syben said. "If Saud hadn't helped out, the camel would have attacked you. It would have ripped you up. Just look at those terrible teeth."

Little Giant danced with rage. "My Professor Sobrinsky suit."

The camel walked away. Saud picked up the suit and offered it to Little Giant. *"Non, non, et non,"* Little Giant screamed, tore off his pith helmet, flung it on the sand, and jumped on top of it.

An Arab brought a burnoose and slid the garment over Little Giant's head. Another wrapped a strip of cloth around his head. Little Giant's eyes stared from behind his round spectacles through the folds of his headgear. Syben and Mark, hands across their mouths, turned away; the Arabs, threatened by Little Giant's fists, stepped back. Mathilde wasn't laughing. She put her arm across his shoulder. "Those exotic clothes look very well on you," Mathilde said. "Now you're a sheikh, too, just like Lawrence of Arabia. It's an honor when they allow you to affect their dress. You really controlled that fierce camel very well. We're going to eat mutton. Can you smell the roasting meat?"

Little Giant walked with her. "With French fries and a tossed salad?"

"And custard pudding afterward," Mathilde said.

CHAPTER 8

A FIRE, fed by Saud and company, was burning between the rocky dwellings. The wood must have been extraordinarily dry, because it caught flame at once, spitting long bright orange tongues of fire that danced frantically and sometimes bolted straight up, licking their fiery way into the darkness. The members of the expedition were squatting on the ground, with the brothers crossed-legged and Mathilde kneeling. The meal consisted, indeed, of mutton, dripping gravy into the parched sand.

Saud sat between Mark and Syben and served his guests, tearing pieces of meat off the bones and passing them on. His hands were dirty and his nails black.

"Shouldn't you instigate the negotiations?" Syben asked.

Mark extracted a piece of yellow fat from his mouth and threw it into the fire. The melting fat hissed furiously. "Right now?"

Syben had swallowed his own lump of fat. He gagged and pressed his hand on his lips.

"Saud?" Mark asked.

"Oui?"

"Le haschisch?"

Saud poured the coffee and broke two lumps of sugar off a solid piece given him by one of his subordinates. He put the two pieces down and held up his hand. Everybody was silent. Only the crackling of the fire remained audible. He knocked the pieces of sugar against each other. A shot cracked in the distance.

"L'haschisch," Saud said, *"est là."*

"I never," Syben said.

Saud rapped a knuckle on Mark's knee.

"*Oui?*" Mark asked.

"*L'argent?*"

"Listen, Syben," Mark said, "even the Swiss do not conduct their dealings in such a sinister manner. Now what? We are thrown together with a mob of muggers peering at us with rats' eyes. The hashish hangs somewhere in the night. Do they really expect me to count down a hundred thousand dollars?"

Saud's knuckles rapped Mark's kneecap again. "*L'argent?*"

"Give it to them," Little Giant said, "and maybe they'll allow us to live for a few more minutes."

Mark looked at Mathilde. "It's your money."

Mathilde shivered. The day's heat had been sucked up by the nude rocks around them, and icy drafts tore through the little warmth the fire was spreading. "Give it to him. He is Achmed's nephew, and Achmed is my brother's trusted partner."

"May the god of finance smile down on me." Mark pulled his attaché case toward him and pressed the little lock. Saud bent over its contents. "*Pour vous,*" Mark said hoarsely. "*Cent paquets de cent; chaque billet est de cent dollars.*"

"Now what are you saying?" Little Giant asked.

"I'm saying that a hundred times a hundred times a hundred is a hundred thousand."

"Is the equation correct?" Little Giant asked.

"Yes," Syben said, "three times two zeroes is six zeroes. No, it isn't. You're giving him too much, Mark."

"Not at all," Mark said, "there are a hundred bundles in the case and each bundle is a thousand dollars."

Mathilde looked into the case. "Ten bundles."

"Only ten?" Little Giant asked. "Then we're not giving him enough. Don't say anything; maybe he won't notice."

Saud was counting. There were ten bundles, and each bundle contained a hundred notes of a hundred dollars each. He counted on his fingers.

"He's having trouble, too," Little Giant said. "It *is* tricky you know? I always get confused, too, when I'm dealing with more than a thousand guilders, and these are dollars; that's something else altogether."

Saud touched his forehead, then his mouth, then his heart. He clicked the case closed and put it down again. He gestured.

"We have to follow him," Mark said. "Come along, Syben. I don't feel like dying alone."

Saud had a flashlight with a long handle. They didn't have to walk far before he raised his arm and signaled: three long flashes, three short, three long.

Little Giant trotted alongside his brothers, lifting his burnoose so that he wouldn't stumble. "That means SOS. Save Our Souls. Very apt. But I don't really care about my soul now. I'd be more than content if I could get my body out in one piece.

A small light answered from the hill.

"*Ils viennent*," Saud said.

Little Giant touched Syben. "I'm happy after all that I came along."

"Why don't you wait till you see what's coming at us?"

"No," Little Giant said, "that's not what I mean. I'd stay scared, even if we were dealing with old aunts instead of dancing dervishes. I mean that I'm finally beginning to understand surrealism. I have all the picture books at home, but the explanations are always in French, and I can't read French. Here, the explanations are also in French, and I still haven't got a clue, but even so, it's all becoming clear to me. Are you following me?"

"Not quite," Mark said.

"I get you," Syben said.

"Syben," Little Giant said, "sometimes you disappoint me. If you really understood, you would keep quiet."

Mark peered at the hills. "Donkeys, a lot of donkeys; there's no end to them and they're all heavily loaded."

The sun came up, and the donkeys slowly descended the steep path, unwilling to respond to the shouting of the boys running alongside.

"A lot of hashish," Mark said.

"Didn't I tell you," Mathilde said when the donkeys had reached the hovel, "that my business contacts are reliable?"

Saud and his men untied the knots that held the jute-covered bales carried by the donkeys. The bales were stacked, and guarded by Arabs with rifles.

"Shouldn't we check the merchandise?" Mark asked. "Who knows what's under the jute? I don't want to risk my life carrying compacted goat droppings all the way to France."

His fist hit one of the bales. Saud stepped forward, inserted his hand into his burnoose, and jerked it back. A curved dagger flashed.

"Choisissez," Saud said. Mark pointed at a bale. The knife slid through the jute cover. Saud pulled out a brown slab, cut off a sliver and offered the sample to Mark. Mark studied the hash.

"Eat it," Syben said, "but give me half."

"And I?" Little Giant asked. "Hash doesn't taste well, but it does cure fear."

The brothers chewed dexterously.

"Is that hashish?" Mark asked. "I only ate it baked into cookies."

"Yes," Syben said.

Saud's eyes drilled into Mark's face.

"Merveilleux," Mark said. *"Très bon."*

Saud took them to one of the cabins and pointed at sheepskins arranged on its dirt floor. *"Maintenant, dormir; nous partons ce soir."*

"Mathilde," Little Giant said in his sleep, "don't do that. Ouch."

"I didn't do anything," Mathilde said from the other corner of the cabin.

"That's a cat," Syben said. "He's been at me, too. He punches and he scratches. Chase him outside."

The cat returned through the window.

Little Giant was bothered by diarrhea and had to leave the cabin. The hashish made his legs feel as though they consisted of tight elastic bands, but he couldn't finish his dance because the seam of his burnoose got caught on his shoe. He rolled until he reached the feet of a guard, who, shaken from his sleep, pointed his rifle.

"Who's snoring?" Mathilde asked.

Syben pushed Mark on his side. Only Syben was resting, motionless on his back, alternately dozing and admiring lines of light playing on the beams that supported the cabin's sagging roof.

The return trip took longer than the way up. The camels carried the merchandise now, and a dozen horsemen accompanied the caravan. The column moved slowly in the face of a raging gale that threw hot sand into the travelers' faces. The moon barely penetrated the swirling dust clouds, and the Europeans were now indistinguishable from their Arab hosts. They all wore burnooses and carried weapons. Syben was armed with a rifle, and Mark and Little Giant had machine pistols, with wooden butts and round magazines attached to their short barrels, strapped to their saddles. When the arms were issued, Saud had commanded them to practice, and the pupils dutifully aimed at straw targets. Little Giant refused at first.

"Part of the game," Syben said.

Little Giant hit his target. Mark didn't. Syben had to teach him to touch the trigger only briefly and to press the barrel down with his other hand.

"I was a first lieutenant," Mark said, "with the Queen's Hussars."

"Try again," Syben said. "The Arabs don't know that."

Apart from the howling of the wind the travelers also heard drumming: short, vibrating beats rolling down from the hills.

"The enemy?" Little Giant asked as the sinister sound accompanied the caravan.

Saud explained. "I believe," Mark said, "that our sheikh wants us to know that the drumming has been caused by a certain Raoul, and that this Raoul is a devil, perhaps the same demon who lives on the mountaintop. The *djebel*. That thundering is probably a sound mirage."

The horseman who had been riding ahead galloped back and spoke to Saud, expressing himself in gutteral exclamations dominated by sharp *g*'s. He waved his binoculars and pointed to the east.

"The cops," Little Giant said. "But we've got nothing on us. Only twenty camels loaded down with dangerous drugs, but the camels lost their way in the desert, happened to attach themselves to us, and we haven't been able to chase them away."

Saud issued orders. His henchmen fanned out. The caravan was moving again, jerkily, until the camels regained their easy swaying gait.

"It can't be the cops," Mathilde said to Mark. "Hashish is okay here. It's probably only the competition."

"It's only the competition," Mark said to Little Giant.

"And they'll shoot at us with blanks?"

Syben was riding on Little Giant's other side. "No, but we'll be allowed to shoot back. This is a free country."

This is another dream, Little Giant thought. I've had them before when I've forgotten to open a bedroom window in my snug little house in the dike. The reports are caused by the farmer's tractor that won't start again because it's a cold morning.

The fighting and the ever-increasing gale slowed the caravan's progress. One of the horsemen came back dead, strapped to his saddle. Saud held up his hand, and the camels knelt down. Saud's men put up tents.

"Where is Little Giant?" Syben asked.

Little Giant lay on his back, his hands crossed on his chest. His eyes were closed.

"Are you ill?" Syben asked.

"I'm dying."

"So how come you're talking so clearly?"

"Because I have to tell you that I have receded into biblical times and have just lived through a passage that I will now explain to you. I'm dying and waiting for the Good Samaritan."

Syben squatted down, slid his arms under Little Giant's body, and lifted his brother up. He put him down again near the fire fed with twigs and horse dung by Saud's horsemen.

"Stay here," Syben said. "I'll get you some whiskey, and there'll be a nice meal in a minute. Amuse yourself; this is true adventure, and we're making a lot of money out of it besides."

Little Giant watched Syben walk away. Morning broke, and the wind finally calmed. Unreal, diffused light filled the enormous cupola of the sky.

Syben's ponytail danced on his back and lengthened into a fold of his burnoose that reached to the ground. Syben's sleeves swayed solemnly. Behind his majestic body the camels waited, hairy, bizarre, colorful silhouettes that fit nowhere in Little Giant's interpretation of the world. Perhaps the hash was still working, because Little Giant felt precariously at ease. That's Christ walking away from me, Little Giant thought happily, or some other youthful archfather.

Mark, leaning against a saddle, watched Syben. He had also been swept from common ground.

Tragedy = Comedy, Mark thought. The dead man just now proves it. He plays the clown, tied astride the horse, flopping his head, flapping his arms, showing me nothing matters much. Mark told himself he felt relieved, not frightened.

Syben sat down between his brothers and passed a bottle.

Alcohol hit their stomachs.

"You were looking just like Christ right now," Little Giant said, "when you walked to your camel."

"My very thought," Mark said.

Little Giant leaned forward so that he could look around Syben. "That's what you thought too, eh?"

"Exactly. The holy prophet, interpreter of multidimensional experience"—Mark lifted an expressive finger—"not trying to be funny now."

"Let's have that bottle," Little Giant said.

"No joke," Mark repeated. "Syben was the messiah there, as shown in picture books at kiddies' school. Stately figure. Well-meaning."

"I do mean well," Syben said.

"No no," Mark said. "You're nothing special, even if you looked okay just now." He laughed. "Let's face it, Syben. We know you, you know. You masturbated as a youngster; maybe you still do now. You stole from Dad's wallet; you lied a lot; you made a mess of everything."

Little Giant gave Syben the bottle. "So did you, Mark. And you were always teasing me because I was a physical misfit and couldn't defend myself very well. I even owe you my name—Little Giant—a nasty label that stuck, because it sounds funny and seems to define the contrast rather well."

Syben drank. Mark pulled the bottle out of Syben's hand and passed it along to Little Giant. "Drink more, and get hold of yourself. It's easy to criticize, but if I hadn't named you, somebody else would have thought of a worse expression. And you're just like everybody else; you're only aware of your own suffering. What do you think of *my* position? Of Dad's three sons, I'm the only real bourgeois, a common denominator from the middle class, with a hidden desire to float up, that has been, up till now, efficiently frustrated. My wife left me because I bored her, and my peers pushed me aside without even taking the trouble to buy me a calculator watch that makes music when you press a button. *You* can always realize your ambitions when you weave your reeds, and in your perversions, that seem to combine with your extraordinary shape. And Syben, of course, is so detached from everything that all he has to do is walk up and down to create a vision."

"When I was in India, I tried to walk on water," Syben said. "I didn't mind sinking, but I hurt my toe on a rusty can, and the wound became badly infected."

"Just a moment," Little Giant said. "I didn't like that bit about my perversions just now, and you can keep your ideas about my extraordinary shape to yourself. What do you mean? Do you want to fight?"

"Put that machine pistol down," Syben said. "When Mark

wants to fight, he'll do it with bad Arabs, not with his own brother. And you do have an extraordinary shape, Little Giant; you turned out a little small, but you should be accustomed to references to that aspect of your outside personality. Would you pass the bottle?"

Little Giant caressed Syben's ponytail. "You've always been kind to me."

"That's what matters," Mark said. "Real kindness matters. I see too little of that. That's why I saw Christ just now, but it turned out to be nothing but Syben again. I have a need for kindness, for true love; surely it must be around somewhere. And sometimes I want to see it, too, especially when I go crazy." He held up his mug.

"Are you crazy?" Little Giant asked.

"Yes," Mark said. "Maybe I used to be normal, although the crazy part must have always been alive in me, but then if you go to work every day and watch TV during the evenings, you don't notice it so much. That I seem to be able to accept the disappearance of the lost million proves my madness, and that I, a gentleman from Rotterdam, am now talking shit in the African desert, while dressed in a sleeping gown, proves it again."

"The lost million," Little Giant said, filling his mug, too. "Let's go into that again. I never stole it, because to do so would be destructive, while it's always been my thing to develop in a creative manner. You have to believe me, because drunken dwarfs speak the truth. That money was suddenly gone and never showed up again, although we turned Dad's apartment completely upside down. I controlled myself then, but I would have preferred to have had a fit on the carpet. Who . . . ?"

"Not me," Mark said, "and the insanity also boiled in me and hasn't simmered down yet. But there was always a lady around and my own brothers, so that I couldn't give vent to my rage properly. I'm drunk, too, now and therefore speaking the truth. I had nothing to do with that despicable theft."

"Are you drunk, too?" Little Giant asked Syben.

Syben pulled the bottle out of his mouth. "Certainly."

"So speak the truth."

Syben screwed the bottle into the sand. "As a spiritual adventurer, it is my task to improve myself, which means the world, continuously."

"Yes, yes," Mark said. "Did you lift the money, or didn't you?"

"I didn't," Syben said. "Would I steal from my own family? From the woman I love?"

"Do you love Mathilde?"

"He can love on forever," Mark said. "Where is Mathilde anyway? If we are innocent, then she must be guilty. Logic applies, even in an insane situation. Four minus three equals Mathilde."

"What do we know about Mathilde?" Little Giant asked. "Except that she's beautiful and that Syben loves her? Dad loved her, too, and suddenly she existed in the Kralingen apartment, vacuumed the carpet, made coffee, and shared his king-size bed. Dad was over seventy by then and never womanized."

Mark pulled the bottle from the sand. "Dad was a gentleman, and when gentlemen indulge themselves, they do so behind impenetrable screens. He wasn't happily married to Mother. He said so himself. To me that confession was no surprise. Who knows the ways in which Dad broke free in secrecy?"

"I remember that you talked very differently not so long ago," Syben said.

"I was neither drunk nor inspired then. And maybe Mathilde is no lady, even if she claims she has been educated in a Swiss private school. Her brother is a gangster."

"Now wasn't *he* a likeable fellow?" Little Giant asked.

Mark shook Syben's arm. "If Mathilde has our million, what are we going to do about it?"

"Keep waiting," Syben said, "and not lose sight of her for a moment."

Little Giant's camel, who had been sniffing the sand on the other side of the fire, lifted its huge head and snorted loudly.

Little Giant raised his voice. "Keep your ugly trap shut."

The Arabs, asleep in a disorderly pattern, woke up and stared at Little Giant.

"Close your nasty, mean little eyes at once," Little Giant screamed.

"There is Mathilde," Syben said. "Don't shout like that; she needs her rest."

"It's stuffy in the tent," Mathilde said, "and I keep dreaming about the poor corpse of that pathetic Arab. How could I know that such terrible risks would be part of my innocent adventure? I'm sending you all to hell, and can only hope that I'll join you there."

"Now now," Mark said, "we're with you, Mathilde. Three blameless knights with your name embroidered on their banners. We'll make sure that you return safely so that you can spend the rest of your life dressing and undressing in your boudoir while we take turns peeping through the keyhole."

"I dreamed," Mathilde said, "that you were the corpse. I saw all three of you melted together in the remains of one valiant warrior. There was more to the dream. I had known you all a long time, and all this had happened before."

The Arabs, with the exception of the guards, were asleep again. The camels and the horses slept, too. The enemies who hadn't been shot or hacked to pieces had gone home. Mathilde squatted between the brothers. One of the guards threw more camel dung in the fire.

"I wish I'd never met you," Mathilde said.

Mark and Little Giant leaned against each other. Their mouths hung open. Mark smacked loudly, and Little Giant snored softly.

"Why would you try to outrun your fate?" Syben asked. "Wouldn't it be better if you accepted your limited choice and explored the possibilities of the given direction?"

"But your father was such a dear man," Mathilde said. "I wanted to rest with him, and the three of you are connected with your father."

"So rest with us. Would you like to sleep in my arms?"

"No," Mathilde said, "I'm going back to the tent, and you can stay here and keep your distance. Up till recently I slept with your father, and the idea of exchanging his memory for a living experience is distasteful."

CHAPTER 9

"WHOA," Little Giant shouted, but Syben kept driving. The truck's bumper pushed over the white-and-red painted wooden barricade that had been put across the road. Boards broke under the truck's wheels, and the policemen who had been behind the fences jumped away. The policemen looked neat, dressed in freshly laundered uniforms, wearing stiff hats secured with leather straps under aggressive chins. Syben increased speed. The truck swerved through the curve.

"Hashish is legal here, and I am Professor Sobrinsky. Weren't those nice cops?"

"Not anymore," Mark said, "because we have broken their fences. Attempted manslaughter on police officers in the line of duty is a serious offense, more heavily punishable in Arabia than in Rotterdam I would think."

"It was the competition again," Syben said, "the enemy. They all had beards. Real cops have no beards here, and I didn't see a police car anywhere, either."

Mathilde opened her window and adjusted the outside mirror. "I don't believe they're coming after us."

Little Giant made himself more comfortable on the hard seat. "From now on I'm not in this anymore. I'm in a foreign country and will be enjoying the view. You're driving too fast, Syben."

The truck leaned into the next curve. "You'll have to put up with this for a while," Syben said, "in case they're coming after us after all." The truck's engine roared. Little Giant closed his eyes.

*   *   *

"Is the professor with us again?" Mark asked Mathilde, walking on a beach later.

Little Giant rushed toward them. "What's keeping Syben?"

Mark flicked his lighter so that he could look at his watch. "That may take a long time. Syben said he would travel by bus to the marina, and buses don't keep to schedules here. Cap Blanc is some distance away." He stuck a finger in his mouth and held it up. "There isn't much wind, so he'll have to use the engine."

"What if the competition-enemy attacks us here meanwhile?" Little Giant asked.

"Never," Mark said. "How can they know what beach we selected?"

"They'll see the truck."

"We hid it, didn't we?" Mathilde asked.

"Those little boys who were here a minute ago had a nasty look on their faces," Little Giant said. "By now they'll be in the bushes mumbling into their walkie-talkies."

"Don't worry."

"Why shouldn't he worry?" Mathilde asked. "Worry as much as you like, Little Giant. I'm nervous, too. I wish I'd never started all this."

"Ouch," Mark said.

"Now what?" Mathilde asked.

"I burned my fingers trying to look at my watch again. The situation is too much for me, too. I understand that we are engaged in changing a quarter of a million into half a million and that an exercise of that order can't be too easy, because if it were, my seven years at university spent in the study of economics would have been lost. Even so . . . Where are those little boys with their walkie-talkies?"

"Gone," Little Giant said, "but they were carrying a bag, and it must have contained a walkie-talkie."

A yacht, with its sails down and its engine puttering quietly, approached the coast.

"Allah be praised," Little Giant said.

"Allah supports the enemy," Mark said.

"Thank him anyway," Mathilde said. "Gods should love us all."

The boat dropped its anchor. They saw Syben, bathed in moonlight, busy near the stern. The anchor chain rattled.

"Can't he come in closer?" Little Giant asked. "How are we going to get all those bales on board?"

Syben rowed to the beach with short strokes of little yellow plastic oars that protruded awkwardly from his inflatable dingy.

"Look at that toy." Mark said. "It'll never hold more than one bale at a time. There and back, there and back. It'll take us all night."

"There and *back*," Little Giant sang.

"Are you that happy?" Mathilde asked.

"I express my positive feelings in song," Little Giant said. "The dream is almost done. I'm sure the dream is good for me, but I don't really enjoy being taught in my sleep, and certainly not in Arabic."

"Good evening," Syben said. "It's lovely on the water, and the boat is in excellent shape."

"Here you are," Mark said. "One bale of hashish."

Mathilde stepped out of her boots and unbuttoned her pants.

"What are you doing?" Mark asked. "I like watching you when you undress, but are you sure this is the right time? We've got a lot of work to do."

Mathilde slipped out of her blouse. "I'll swim to the yacht so that I can help Syben by pulling up the bales; it'll save time."

Little Giant sat on the beach.

"And what about you?" Mark asked. "You should be carrying bales."

"I shouldn't be anything at all," Little Giant said. "If, by accident, a dream contains pleasant happenings, the dreamer should take the time to enjoy them. Maybe I'll be buried in the sand in a minute, with only my head sticking out, smeared full of honey by the enemy in order to attract flesh-eating ants, but I haven't gotten to that part yet. What's up now is a

view of a well-made woman displaying herself on a North
African beach, about to dive into the crashing waves so that
she may be even more beautiful when the spray dapples her
naked skin."

"Stop leering," Mark said, "and longing."

"So what are you doing?" Little Giant asked without turning his head.

"I'm leering and longing."

"Get to work," Little Giant shouted as he ran to the truck.
He trotted back holding a bale above his head.

Mark ran to the truck, too.

The inflatable dinghy manned by Syben made a great
number of trips.

"Last bale." Mark said, "Now for the baggage and Mathilde's
clothes."

"We can leave those here," Syben said.

"No," Little Giant said. "Her brother is waiting on the
other side and is a gangster who employs a butler with a
broken nose and a bulge under his armpit. His Doberman
pinschers lurk in the garden. A tough guy like that won't
appreciate us raping his sister."

Syben took the bags and Mathilde's clothes. Little Giant
watched the dinghy climbing another wave. Syben's teeth
gleamed in the moonlight. "He's enjoying himself," Little
Giant said. "Doesn't he ever get scared?"

"He does," Mark said, "but he shows it differently. He's
become primitive again because he's been out of civilization
for some years. Apes also show their teeth when they're
scared."

CHAPTER 10

A CLEAN, white yacht, recently manufactured, its mainsail tight, its jibs standing out firmly, cut through fresh waves slapping smartly against the bow. The sky was blue and so was the sea. A lean man with a white cap daintily in balance on his blond curls held the helm; a lovely lady in the smallest of bikinis lay on the cabin roof, one leg stretched out, one leg bent; a bearded little fellow sat near the bow, and a third man leaned against the mast. The North African coast was still visible as a wavy yellow line, perpendicular to the foamy wake of the *Annabelle*. The vessel's services were legally chartered, properly paid for and insured, and its cargo was neatly stowed fore and aft.

The yacht had the sea to itself, with the exception of some gulls gliding along and a triangular sail still close to the coast but steadily increasing in size.

"Hey," Little Giant yelled.

"Yes?" Syben asked.

"Over there," Little Giant shouted.

Mark brought binoculars. Syben looked. "That is a dhow," Syben said, "an Arab boat. Dhows are slender craft and carry a lot of sail. They may be somewhat outdated, but they're considerably faster than this here tub."

Mathilde stood next to Syben, shading her eyes while she took in the view. "Oh my God."

Mark looked, too. "There is a cannon on the stern manned by a crew of Arabs in dirty party dresses."

"Could I have the binoculars again?" Syben asked.

"Well?" Mark asked Syben.

"No cannon, but a machine gun set on a tripod."

"Shouldn't there be an end, even to calamity?" Little Giant asked. "The wind is down; perhaps they have no engine."

Syben pushed a button, and the *Annabelle* trembled. He adjusted a handle. The *Annabelle* began to shake.

Little Giant bent over the railing next to the rudder. "Shouldn't the propeller be turning?"

"Isn't it turning?"

"It isn't."

"Then something isn't right," Syben said. "Why don't you all sit down out of my way. I'll lift up these boards so I can get at the shaft."

"The engine is going," Little Giant said, "so something is happening, but it would be nice if the propeller turned, too."

Syben knelt. "A bolt has vibrated out of the connection, which means there isn't any."

"Any what?"

"Any connection." Syben smiled at his brother. "That's the principle of machines, everything should be together."

"I've never been too technical," Little Giant said. "You think you can fix it, whatever it is?"

"If I had some tools."

Mark found an adjustable wrench, and Syben tried to get hold of the bolt. The wrench kept slipping. Syben kept trying. The dhow moved closer.

"I believe that that machine gun isn't working, either," Little Giant said peering through the binoculars. "They're applying tools to it, too."

Syben put down the wrench. "This thing doesn't work; what else have we got?"

Mathilde found a pair of pliers. Its grooved beak grabbed hold of the bolt. "Right," Syben said. "This should give us some action. Is the propeller turning now?"

Little Giant hung over the railing again. "Not quite."

"Must be the nut," Syben said. "The threads are stripped. Perhaps I can insert a bit of cloth."

"When I was a lieutenant with the Queen's Hussars," Mark said, "I took a course in strategy. If you can't avoid the enemy in one way, there are always other ways, but right now I wouldn't have any idea as to what they could be."

"That rattling," Little Giant said, "means that they're firing the gun, and those flashes on the water are probably bullets."

"Now," Syben said. The propeller turned, and the *Annabelle* pushed ahead, helped along by a gust of wind filling her sails.

"Shouldn't we take cover?" Mathilde asked.

"We could lie down," Syben said, "but it won't do much for us. They're using a fifty-caliber Russian machine gun, and its bullets will pierce concrete. This boat is made of Fiberglas."

"Very nice," Little Giant said. "We are going faster than they are. We're out of range." A salvo from the dhow hit the *Annabelle*; the cabin door fell apart. Mark's teeth rattled. Little Giant began to cry. Mathilde embraced her legs and rested her head on her knees.

"My cap," Syben said. "They shot off my cap."

The wind strengthened. Night fell, and a light fog settled down on the waves. The dhow was out of sight.

"You think we've lost them?" Mark asked an hour later.

"They must have gone back." Syben said. "We're getting close to Sardinia and the Italian coast guard."

Syben and Mark took turns steering the boat, but Syben spent more time at the rudder because Mark was suffering from severe trembling. "I'll never try this again," Mark said when he passed the helm to Syben. "There are too many intangibles; it's impossible to plan an adventure like this well. Greed has interfered with my intelligence."

"Cheer up," Syben said, his foot on the helm. "A little adventure won't harm anybody. And this is ending well; we'll see the French coast day after tomorrow."

"Hashish," Mark said, "is a malicious herb. The *djebel* on the mountain and Raoul, the desert's wicked drummer—we had plenty of warnings. The money was a curse, the curse of my father."

"Our father," Syben said, "was a kindly man. Why don't you make some coffee?"

Mark brought the coffee. Light returned to the sky, and low clouds were colored by the still-invisible sun. The wind was increasing, and the vessel pushed up a bright bow wave. "Ha," Syben shouted.

"A curse," Mark mumbled, "my father's curse: money and a beautiful woman. First she steals half, and then she drags us into deadly drug dealing."

"Oh, really," Syben said, "you're sailing on the Mediterranean in good company and on a lovely yacht. Enjoy yourself a little, will you?"

"Her brother is no good, either."

"One of the nicest men I ever met."

"Listen here," Mark said, "her brother is waiting somewhere outside the apartment building. Little Giant is asleep on the couch, soaked in genever. You and I are passed out in the spare room. Mathilde sneaks into the sitting room, grabs the million, and throws it out of the window. Her brother catches the parcel. Then she thinks of the hash adventure, inspired probably by her brother's advice, and means to be rid of us once and for all. What do you think would have happened if that dhow had got hold of us? Wouldn't she have been treated politely while we were mashed up for fish food?"

"Mathilde cast in the devil's role," Syben said. "Not really impossible, because she's too beautiful for a human, but there should be logic even in a devil's plan. Why would she lift one million if there were two available? And why would she stay with us? She could have gone away; with two million you can go away forever."

Little Giant fought his way out of the cabin.

"There are jute threads all through your beard," Syben said. "Did you sleep well?"

"No," Little Giant said, "those bales are shifting, and there is a lot of water in the cabin. The boat is leaking."

Mathilde joined them. "Do you know that there are holes in the boat's side? There is a lot of water in the hold."

The machine-gun bullets had torn open the vessel's port side. Syben steered the *Annabelle* through the wind, but the water flowed to the lee side and the yacht heeled over dangerously.

"Couldn't we bail?" Mark asked. "Is there a pump, maybe?"

"We're down too far already," Syben said. "We'll have to get rid of the cargo."

"Never," Mark said. "Why don't you take us over there; that seems like a nice blue patch."

"The sea's color doesn't matter all that much," Syben said. "The waves will be just as high."

Mark jumped up and down. "It's bluer out there because there's less wind. That's called calm; are you familiar with the term? *Calm?*"

A sudden gust of wind chopped up the blue patch.

"Turn her into the wind!" Little Giant screamed. "I'll get the mainsail down."

The rope slipped through his hands. The sail came down too fast, and the boom hit Mark's shoulder. Little Giant's arm got caught, and the halyard pulled him off the deck. Syben let go of the helm and pulled Little Giant down by the legs. Mark groaned on a bench and massaged his shoulder. Little Giant blew on the torn skin of his arm.

"Away with the cargo," Syben said, "before you all get wounded too badly. Give us a hand."

"Now we can see where the leaks are," Mathilde said, once both cabins and the hold had been emptied. "How about twisting some pieces of cloth to fill in the holes?"

Their subsequent activity as they tried to plug the leaks, mainly with underwear supplied by Mathilde, increased the leaking because they used too much force. Crumbling plastic broke away under their hands. The water level in the boat rose steadily.

Syben handed out life jackets, and Mathilde attached white towels to paddles.

"Who should I wave to?" Little Giant asked. "There's nobody around."

"Out there," Syben said. "There goes a cruise ship."

They waved, but the ship was too far away and not paying attention. It never wavered from its course, and the sea became empty again.

"Do something," Little Giant said to Syben.

Syben sat on the main cabin roof, his legs tucked into each other, his eyes half-closed.

"What's he doing?" Little Giant whispered to Mark.

"He is meditating SOS signals," Mark whispered to Little Giant.

"He looks awful," Mathilde whispered. "That life jacket makes him quite ridiculous. The color is wrong, too; yellow doesn't go with his golden locks."

The wind seemed to be gaining in strength.

"Stop that," Mark shouted. "You're making things worse."

Syben freed his legs and lay down. His efforts might have been useful after all, because they were saved later during the day by a fishing boat out of Corsica. Most of the bales of hashish had floated away and disappeared behind towering waves. The fisherman managed to find two when he circled the *Annabelle* before tying on.

"Can't I tell him that the merchandise belongs to us?" Mark asked.

Little Giant studied their savior, a wide-shouldered, short-set man who stared back nastily. "He looks even meaner than Saud."

"He's going to considerable trouble to save us," Syben said, "and should be recompensed. Besides, we're in Italian waters now. If we claim the cargo, we're in trouble."

"Let's see, now," Mark said. "We started off with two million, but one million somehow blew out of a window in Kralingen, and now a quarter of a million gets drowned in the Mediterranean. According to my calculation, that leaves us with three-quarters of a million."

"Still quite a lot," Little Giant said, "seven hundred and fifty thousand living coins. Isn't life known for its potential to multiply?"

"Very true," Syben said. "Please don't look so sad, Mathilde." He touched his back pocket. "The idea that our plan might fail did occur to me before we set out, and I remembered to bring along my savings. As soon as we are ashore, it will buy us white sheets and warm baths."

"I want to go home," Little Giant said.

"It'll buy us airplane tickets, too. There is five thousand in my wallet."

That evening, comfortably seated on rocking chairs in the rear garden of the best hotel in Caregasa, Corsica's holiday resort, the company reflected on the future while listening to cicadas singing in the rosebushes.

"I've lost my share," Mathilde said. "As soon as we're back in Rotterdam, I will leave you."

Mark, considerably cheered by wine and sudden security, thought that the loss should be divided among all parties.

"And the curse?" Syben asked.

"What curse? Poor Mathilde; it was her plan, but we were all committed."

"There, you see Mathilde?" Little Giant asked. "We're still doing well; we were only broke for a moment, but we're all rich again all of a sudden."

Mark delivered a lecture on Shared Fear that creates Deep Friendship. He proposed that greed could lead to suffering but that courage would cut through bourgeois pettiness. He mentioned his own limitations but promised, in various formulations, that he would improve the quality of his future endeavors. False starts often lead to the ultimate realization of supreme ideals. "*Supreme,*" Mark said.

"Do you mind if I go to bed?" Mathilde asked. "I'm tired and should be punished."

The three brothers got up and sat down again. "Why should she be punished?" Little Giant asked.

Mark raised his glass. "Because she thinks herself stupid." He smiled. "And maybe she is, which could be a good thing for us, for if we had considered her suggestion on its merits, without being blinded by her beauty, we might never have found ourselves in this exotic part of the world."

Syben stretched and groaned happily. "You're right. This seems like an excellent spot. Why don't we stay awhile?"

"Good luck comes," Mark said, "to those who keep on trying. We must go on."

"Where now?" Little Giant asked.

"America," Mark said.

"What would we do in America?"

"Make money."

"Maybe nobody told you," Syben said, "but the gold that one could pick up on American streets has been picked up awhile ago."

"It's still on the tarmac. I have friends out there who are very good at grabbing untold wealth, and the methods they use are well known to me."

"So what would these friends be doing?" Syben asked.

"They invest in valuable documents."

Little Giant grabbed his glass. "I've heard enough. More suffering ahead."

"You will be joining us, I trust?"

"Of course," Little Giant said, "I don't want to bore you by repeating myself forever, but one of us disposed of an illegally obtained million. As long as it doesn't show, we'll stay together."

"Gambling with shares," Syben said, "you're sure that's the right thing to do?"

Mark patted Syben's shoulder. "Leave it to me; it's about time that a professional took over. But first we have to go home to pick up more cash. I will refill our coffers."

NEW YORK

CHAPTER 11

GUSTS of icy wind cut through Forty-second Street and tore at the little group of shivering travelers. The cabdriver misunderstood Mark's explanation and put them off at the corner of Fifth Avenue. He pointed both forward and to the rear, *"Aquí, los hoteles."*

"I thought they spoke English in America," Mathilde said. "Can I carry my own suitcase? Give it to me, Little Giant; you've got enough baggage. What's in the plastic bag?"

"Dad's stamp albums."

Syben looked through the narrow street. "There are some ten hotels here; what was ours called again?"

"Mohawk," Mark said.

"Over there." Little Giant walked ahead. "A Mohawk is an Indian, and there's a suspended head with feathers, in neon. You know how I know that?"

"That Indians wear feathers?"

"No, that a Mohawk is an Indian? I learned that from the stamps, 1922 series, the fourteen shent."

"You're lisping."

"I'm not lisping."

"You are, you said 'shent' instead of 'cent.' "

"That's what I should be saying," Little Giant said, "in America they put a stroke through the *c*."

"Keep going," Mark shouted. "There's too much wind here. The sooner we're inside, the better; the Mohawk is one of New York's most expensive hotels, and luxury will be awaiting us." Syben walked behind Mark, arm in arm with Mathilde. Mark beckoned impatiently.

"Don't rush me," Syben said. "This is my first proper look at America, and I'm enjoying myself."

"Truly?" Mathilde asked.

"Just a little. That flying wasn't too pleasant. We were like squeezed herrings in a cask, and that cab would have been junked three years ago in any civilized country."

"This is the richest land in the world."

"Revealing itself to us as a dingy slum."

A long line of waiting guests moved slowly towards the counter in the lobby. Mark and Little Giant shuffled along with the others. Little Giant looked at the interior of the hall. "Is this place really expensive?"

"It is. Three hundred dollars a day just for the rooms, breakfast not included and tax added, but it's free to you. You're my guest."

"Worn-out velvet," Little Giant said, "like in an old-fashioned brothel, with worn-out middle-aged prostitutes displayed on couches. Cigar burns on the carpets. The ceiling sags. Or," Little Giant continued, "Aunt Marie's house in a back street of the old section of The Hague, but she had a lovely collection of delft blue pots, and what they're displaying here is imitation Chinese." He left the line, walked over to a shelf in the rear of the lobby, and came back again. "And most of it is cracked and glued."

The man behind the counter suffered from a skin disease and had a glass eye.

"And where are we going now?" Little Giant asked.

"To the elevator."

Squeaking loudly, the elevator came down, and its metal door rattled as a toothless attendant pushed it open. "This is no elevator," Syben said. "This is a mechanical cage for overage parrots."

"If you don't like it here," Mark said, while they followed a uniformed cripple pushing a cart that hung over to one side, "you can find something better yourselves. This was the best choice the travel agency had available."

"I'd like to go for a walk," Syben said. "Coming, Mathilde?"

Mathilde looked at her watch. "It's four A.M. Dutch time. I'm going to bed."

"You come along," Syben said in the room he shared with Little Giant.

Little Giant sat with a stamp album open on his thighs. "What do you have in mind?"

"I believe this is the neighborhood where real jazz still exists."

"That'll cost money."

"Aren't we rich?"

"Mark has our money, and he's in a bad mood."

"I still have some of my own."

"No, you've been paying enough." Little Giant checked his wallet. "A hundred dollars?"

"That'll keep us going for a few hours."

The brothers returned to the narrow street, watching ragged clouds of steam wafting up from cast-iron grates set in the peeling tarmac. An old woman in a torn army overcoat that reached to her bare feet spoke kindly to Syben from under her hat, adorned with broken plastic flowers.

"Madame?" Syben asked.

"I'm not a panhandler," the woman said again, "but I'm badly in need of some cash."

"I do believe she is crazy." Little Giant said.

"What do you think of the gent over there?" Syben asked. The gent was tall and black. He wore a white suit under his bearskin coat, and a shirt of pink lace. He held up a walking stick, peered at its polished silver knob, and conversed with whatever he saw in the knob, intermittently whispering and shouting, and seemed to be supplied with answers to which he listened attentively.

Little Giant wanted to keep watching, but Syben pulled him away.

A young woman in a tweed skirt and matching jacket approached them with short, energetic steps. She stopped in front of Little Giant and bent her knees so that she could look into his eyes. "Hi, dwarf."

"Syben?" Little Giant said.

"Do *you* know," the lady asked slowly, "that I see my analyst at two o'clock every fucking afternoon?"

"Syben?" Little Giant said.

The young lady walked away.

"This is a large city," Syben said, "filled with tensions." He walked to a blue-helmeted policeman twirling his night-stick and standing next to his horse. "Excuse me," Syben said, "do you know if there is an establishment around here where we can listen to some jazz?"

"No," the policeman said. "Keep going; you're blocking my view."

An old man stepped out of the shadow of a doorway. He held up a flat bottle. "Would the gentlemen care for a nip?"

"No thank you."

"Are the gentlemen looking for a jazz club?"

"We are."

"I will direct you," the old man said, "but you'll have to hold on to me because if you don't, I'll fall over."

The club wasn't far.

"Why was the color of that man's skin blue?" Little Giant asked.

"Because he lives on methylated spirits."

"I believe," Little Giant said, when they had settled on stools facing a rickety bar, "that we have managed to reach hell, not that I mind. I've always believed that hell exists, but faith is hard to maintain if theories are not kept up by facts."

A fat man played the trumpet on a stage next to the bar.

"Sssh," Syben said. "Listen."

Little Giant wasn't listening. He looked at the barmaid, whose T-shirt was too small for her. Large pink nipples were painted on the tight, white cotton.

The trumpet engaged in a duet with a saxophone. The trumpet asked, and the saxophone answered. Both trumpeter and sax player were dressed in stained and torn clothes, but the drummer wore a clean suit. His hair was greased down, and a fresh tulip graced his buttonhole. He had only one drum.

The music lasted for a few minutes more.

Syben had frozen in contemplation.

"Syben?" Little Giant asked.

"What you heard just now," Syben said, "is quite impossible. I'm glad I came to the United States. This type of art is only performed here. That was a blues, and blues are supposed to be sadly depressing, but the music was free of all definitions."

"You liked it, eh?" Little Giant said.

"Another drink?" the girl with the nipples asked.

"Yes, please," Syben said. "No, I didn't like it. Or dislike it, for that matter. I tell you, the ultimate performance of anything is no longer limited by our shallow perception. I was taken out of it, Little Giant, but under ordinary circumstances the resulting feeling cannot be described. As long as you think in terms of this or that, you're caught in duality and out of reach of truth. Only when definitions are no longer necessary can the ultimate be realized. I was *there*, just for a moment."

"You are full of it sometimes," Little Giant said, "as I pointed out to you in Tunisia, just a little while ago."

Little Giant listened, too, as the music got even better. Time passed quickly. The club closed.

Two young women were waiting outside and came running along cheerfully to ask if Syben and Little Giant would care to accompany them to their home. "Do come," the young women said. "We live close by, and our apartment is cozy, and so are we."

One woman put her arm around Little Giant's shoulders, and the other played with Syben's ponytail. When she tried to kiss his cheek, Syben hit her chest with his elbow and slapped her hands aside. He ran after the other woman and grabbed her by the collar of her coat. The woman screamed for help. Syben showed her his fist. "Give here."

"*Now* what's happening?" Little Giant asked when Syben came back.

"Pickpockets. Yours got your wallet; mine was a little slow. There you are."

"I never noticed; how come you did?"

"Because I was a mercenary in Chad," Syben said, "and knelt at the feet of a master in the Punjab. The sergeant and the swami agree that one should always pay attention because things are not always what they seem to be."

"I see," Little Giant said.

Mark stood in the hotel lobby talking to two long-haired men in jeans and leather jackets. He greeted his brothers. "Sit down a minute. I'll be joining you."

"What happened?" Little Giant asked.

"I was looking for you two. I went downstairs because you weren't in your rooms. A man with a gun was waiting for me in the elevator."

"Were you robbed?"

"No," Mark said, "because I left my money in my room, but the man wouldn't believe me. He pushed the barrel of his gun into my mouth."

Little Giant shook his head.

"Yes, and I complained at the counter. Those men I was talking to were detectives. They told me to be more careful."

Sirens howled in the street.

"I wish I was back on my camel," Little Giant said, "I felt much safer then. Do you think I can go to bed now?"

CHAPTER 12

"THERE is a copper pipe above my bed," Little Giant said, "that is the home of a gas bubble. The gas bubble entertains a relationship with another who visits her once every hour. When the bubbles make love, they rattle, and when they have a climax, the whole room tinkles."

"There was a cockroach in my slipper," Mathilde said.

"If you don't like it here . . ." Mark said.

"The environment has meanwhile changed again," Syben said. "Look about you, Little Giant. You are having breakfast in a room that, according to the leaflet we were given at the counter, has been declared a national monument and regularly serves as a backdrop for interviews with movie stars and others who have managed to make a success of their lives."

"Yes," Mark said, "the furniture is rococo, and not of the antique, rotted variety but reasonably brand-new. The colors have been limited to simple whites and reds. The waiters all had a haircut yesterday and have wound sashes around their uniforms. An artist arranged the dishes with fruits on the sideboards."

"I am not blind," Little Giant said.

"So read the menu. Would you care for pastries filled with shrimp ragout? Or kidney stew, perhaps? An avocado salad?"

Little Giant ate. Mark looked at Mathilde. Mathilde had finished her soft-boiled egg and was drinking coffee. She listened when anybody said something and answered whenever she was asked a question. She was simply dressed and hadn't quite buttoned her blouse.

"Mark?" Mathilde asked, lifting the coffee carafe.

Mark was fascinated by the dark stream that connected his cup and the carafe's silver spout. Mathilde poured cream into his cup and unwrapped two cubes of sugar. She arranged the cubes so that one stood on the other. Mark watched the sugar dissolve slowly.

"Thank you," Mark muttered.

She pays attention to my needs, Mark thought. She knows how much cream, how much sugar. She cares? Sure, why not? Is she aware of my presence? Obviously, yes. Does my presence excite her? He didn't think it did. Even so. Perhaps.

The possibility made him leer. He vocalized the leer. "Heh, heh."

Little Giant spread butter on toast. He had accidentally felt Mathilde's leg under the table with his own. He could pursue the contact. He did not.

That Mathilde was approachable Little Giant knew better than Mark, but she wasn't completely approachable; he knew that, too. He couldn't hold her hand, for instance, or kiss her suddenly on her neck. He could only get close to her if he manipulated the situation when she wasn't aware.

Syben looked into Mathilde's calm green eyes, through the smoke of her cigarette. If I go all out, Syben thought, I'll have her, but not for very long. The contact won't outlast the duration of the embrace. What I have tried so far was insufficient, although she did react. To push ahead roughly has never been my way. Anything that I have ever lived through pleasantly was given to me by fate in a roundabout way. I'll have to keep trying to do my best and be ready, so that the right moment won't pass me by.

Mark wiped his mouth with his napkin. A waiter brought the check. Mark signed the little form, paying artistic attention to the S of "Sobryne."

"Right," Mark said. "To work."

"How?" Little Giant asked.

Mark checked his watch. "Van Putte is expecting me. His office is around the corner. We studied together in Amsterdam and later worked for the same firm for a while, but Van

Putte wanted to get rich, so he moved to New York. He's a stockbroker now and exceedingly wealthy."

"Do I have to go, too?"

"You don't," Mark said. "You've got some egg on your beard, and I don't think we should expose Van Putte to Syben's ponytail just yet, but if Mathilde would like to join me, I would certainly appreciate the company."

"I don't know anything about documents," Mathilde said.

"Any intelligence won't be wanted," Little Giant said. "Your presence will be required in your function as a nice-looking doll. Americans are easily impressed by success, and whoever has you on a leash can't be a loser."

"Right," Syben said. "Just keep staring at Van Putte so that he'll lose his cool and will divulge some good tips."

"Can you do that?" Little Giant asked, "act like a puppet?"

Mathilde stood up slowly, moving as if she'd been assembled from wooden parts. She turned her head shakily.

"Pull up your skirt," Little Giant said, "while we screen you so that the common crowd won't see anything."

Mathilde was out of view of the other guests. She bent to the side with the same mechanical rhythm and lowered her right hand until it touched her skirt's hem. Her hand came up again pulling the skirt. The top of one black stocking became visible and, afterward, a garter on a smooth white thigh.

"Let's have just a tiny little tad of a bit more," Syben said.

"No," Mathilde said, "I haven't been programmed for subtleties."

Mathilde sat down again. "So how much are you going to gamble now?" Little Giant asked.

Mark calculated on his napkin. "You're not using the correct terminology, because we won't be taking intangible risks. Stockbrokers make use of computer screens that indicate the fluctuation of shares and bonds. I've always been good with figures and can feel their mutual relationships. Besides, economics is my professional field, and I'm familiar with the names of all important firms and commodities. Each figure will give me the meaning of all the others."

"Is that your stake?" Little Giant asked, reading the amount that Mark had written down. "All you have?"

"Yes."

"And when it's gone, it's gone?"

"It won't be gone; it'll be more. Whoever knows how to float on the waves of value will be rich very quickly."

"Please get rich very quickly," Little Giant said. "Meanwhile I'll visit a few postage-stamp dealers. The doorman here also collects stamps and has told me where to go."

Mark got up and offered Mathilde his arm. Syben watched the couple walk away.

"Well?" Little Giant asked.

"Oh, oh, oh," Syben said.

CHAPTER 13

"A HUNDRED thousand dollars?" Little Giant asked without looking up.

"What are you doing?" Syben asked.

Little Giant held up booklets. "I'm studying. These are mail order catalogs showing photographs of postage stamps and quoting prices. I'm comparing prices."

"You're enjoying that?"

"I am, especially because nothing tallies." Little Giant pushed a booklet under Syben's nose. "Look, here is a stamp featuring a zeppelin, for sale for a hundred dollars." He pushed the other booklet under Syben's nose, "And here, somebody else shows the same stamp, featuring the same zeppelin, but this dealer wants a hundred and sixty dollars. Both copies are used and lightly postmarked, but the one costs more than the other. Now why would that be?"

"Fascinating," Syben said. "But did you hear what I said just now? I said that Mark, our Mark, our very own brother Mark, made a hundred thousand dollars. Now that is more than the difference between two identical motorized inflatable balloons."

Little Giant rolled off the bed. Syben stood at the window and watched the view that wasn't there. Their room looked out on the inside of an air shaft that sliced up between concrete walls.

"Gambling on shares?" Little Giant asked.

"Gambling on shares," Syben said. He caressed the telephone on the night table. "That was Mark just now, who passed the good news and invited us for a drink. He's sitting downstairs with Mathilde and Van Putte. I waited a little before informing you because I didn't want to disturb you and preferred to analyze the news. It can't be, I thought, because we've only been four days in New York, and nobody can be that lucky that fast. But maybe Mark can. Shall we go downstairs?"

Van Putte was a thin man with brown curly hair and kind brown eyes. He wore a tweed suit and smoked a pipe. He got up so that Mark could introduce him.

"My brother Syben," Mark said. "And my brother Little Giant."

"There is something to celebrate," Van Putte said. "What would you like to drink?"

"Yes," Mark said. "Ha-ha. It is unbelievable what you can do here if you're really clever. Ha-ha. It just takes a little while before you know what's going on."

"Your brother has done very well," Van Putte said.

"Beginner's luck?" Syben asked.

"No, you can't quite put it that way. Mark has played the game according to its rules."

"Ha-ha," Mark said. "But you were looking over my shoulder, Van Putte. And you had been showing me what happens on your teletype screen."

"Mathilde was looking over your shoulders, too?" Little Giant asked.

"No," Mathilde said, "but I got to go out now and then to buy sandwiches."

Mark's hand touched Mathilde's knee. "You were a great support." Mathilde readjusted her skirt over her knee.

Mark pulled a notepad from the side pocket of his jacket and removed the cap from a ballpoint pen. "Look."

His audience looked.

Mark wrote down figures. "Pay attention. You thought, of course, that I'd just been playing around, but I know the money market's secret script."

Mark took his time writing the formula: 66 ⅛ 48 ⅜ IBM 3.44 5.4 11 4916 64 ⅝ 64 ⅛ -¾.

He underlined the code.

"Yes?" Little Giant asked.

Van Putte pointed at the figures with his pipe. He nodded. "Very well done, Mark. You must have a phenomenal memory."

Mark grinned. "Yes, but you should be in shirtsleeves and rainbow suspenders now, and shout a lot, like your assistant does when he watches the money screen."

"Screen?" Syben asked.

"Like on a TV, but this is a computer. All far too much for you. Too neat and too profound—the mathematical magic will pass you by. Only I can see it."

Little Giant's index finger pointed at the row of figures. "And what may this mean?"

"This means that the magic is within the superior understanding, and consists of tangible material; the figure 66 ⅛ is the highest value of the past fifty-two weeks, and 48 ⅜ the lowest. The name of the stock is IBM. The figure 3.44 is an amount in dollars and represents the last paid dividend." Mark's flat hand hit the paper. "And 5.4 is the percentage, 5.4 percent. This is the yield, very important. And eleven?"

"I did look at a book on the cabala once," Syben said, "the Jewish magic of figures, and eleven was supposed to be off; it's the lunatic's symbol."

Mark waved away the remark. "Not at all. Nonsense. That is the PIE, sir, *price/earnings ratio*. That's what it's all about. Then you know what you have in your hand when you take the plunge. A very nice PIE. Eleven. Yes."

"Is *pie* not just another word for cake?" Mathilde asked.

"No, no, no. No cake. A much-used measure next to the actual value." Mark talked on hurriedly. "And as for 4916, add two zeroes to that, and you know how many shares have changed ownership in a day; and 64 ⅝ is the highest value today and 64 ⅛ was the lowest, and at the same time the final value. Now do you understand why I didn't buy any IBM? The stock is completely uninteresting at present.

"And negative ¾?" Syben asked.

"It went down yesterday," Mark said triumphantly. Three-quarters of a dollar down. When I saw that, I backed off conclusively."

"That's what you were working with?" Little Giant asked, "with that particular formula?"

"No," Mark said, "I chose another way, but I could have worked with it, of course. There are all sorts of ways in which you can net a cool hundred thousand."

The waiter brought the drinks. I would have preferred tea, Little Giant thought. Why am I drinking so much? I'm drinking every day now; how can that be?

"Your health," Syben said. "Now tell me about the hundred thousand dollars. I'm all ears."

"Ha-ha," Mark said.

'Is that what you do, too?" Syben asked Van Putte. "Gamble with shares?"

"Not any more," Van Putte said, "I once did. The first years I was here I did nothing else, but then I had to interrupt my work and spend time pumping gas. Later I tried again and did somewhat better, but I had to stop again because my peptic ulcer broke. Since I started my own brokerage firm, I only give advice, and live on commissions."

That man is rich, Little Giant thought. He lives in a brownstone castle surrounded by a park. He drives a square black car and reads world literature at night, in leather-bound books that have been arranged and sorted by color on mahogany shelves on both sides of his fireplace.

"Well," Mark said. "Ha-ha. This is the way I made the hundred thou. So Van Putte is the stockbroker and knows everybody, and a colleague who owes him a favor passes the information that two large firms are going to merge."

"Like that time in Rotterdam," Little Giant asked, "when two firms joined, and you were fired?"

"What's that?" Mark asked. "Oh, yes, ha-ha. So two firms merged. A intends to buy B, but B finds out, so its owners begin to buy the shares of their own firm."

"But that's done very quietly," Van Putte said, "arranged most discreetly, because otherwise the value of the shares will rise very quickly. A is also buying B's shares, and that factor will accelerate the process. A's and B's stockbrokers are told to collect the loot, but in small parcels, to keep the price on an acceptable level."

"But," Mark interrupted, "you never know whether such a tip is correct, because the market is always alive with talk. People spread a lot of rumors, and you've got to make sure that the information is correct."

"So what do we do?" Van Putte said. "We check our list of clients until we find somebody who owns some B shares and advise him to sell."

"You mean you advise him to buy," Little Giant said, "because you're expecting the price to go up."

"No, ha-ha," Mark said, "we want to make quite sure that the price is going up. Rumors by themselves lead only to suspicions. Suspicions don't pay. It could very well be that nobody wants to buy B."

"Or maybe they do," Van Putte said, "and we'll find out in this way. What happened? As soon as my client offered his shares, they were bought at once."

"Right," Mark said. "Snapped up, ha-ha. But Van Putte tried again, by advising another client to sell. And once again!"

"The price went up?" Little Giant asked.

"Somewhat," Van Putte said, "sufficiently to confirm the rumor."

"But didn't you give your clients bad advice?" Syben asked. "Weren't they selling shares that would appreciate considerably if they held on to them?"

"A stockbroker cannot always give good advice," Mark said. "He's only human, and I happened to be in Van Putte's office, sitting next to him, I, his personal friend."

Van Putte filled his pipe.

"And so you bought in quantity?" Syben asked Mark.

If he says "ha-ha" again, Little Giant thought, if he says "ha-ha" just once again . . .

"Yes," Mark whispered, "I bought with everything I had. Risk it all; if you're working that way, you can't afford to be tight. A handful of aces, and the joker is in as well. And it turned out right. A hundred thousand dollars profit."

Syben stretched his leg. "Very strange shares. You only had about a hundred and twenty-five thousand to spend. I didn't know that the prices of shares fluctuated that much."

"They were very normal shares," Van Putte said, "and the profit per share wasn't out of the way, but Mark was buying on margin, of course; to realize such a large profit, you have to put in ten times as much as he had."

"How could he have put in more than he had?" Little Giant asked.

"Didn't I do well?" Mark said. "Buying on margin?"

"You only put in a small part of what was required? And what if the price had gone down?" Little Giant asked.

"Then he would have lost his stake," Van Putte said. "That's always a possibility, but in this case the risk was small. If the price had gone down, it wouldn't have gone down too steeply, and Mark could have gotten out again without losing all at once."

Little Giant jumped up. His arms swept above the table. Syben protected the glasses from falling over. "Let's get out of here, right now, while the loot is safe."

"Never," Mark said.

"Even so," Van Putte said as he was leaving, "your brother's proposal seems fair to me, Mark. This wasn't just a matter of luck, because the tip was sound and I was backing you, but once you've made a killing like this, it's usually better to get out of the game for a while."

"Ha-ha," Mark said.

CHAPTER 14

"ANOTHER ten thousand dollars gained," Mark said, "even more simply than last time, and without Van Putte. Who says that money doesn't grow on the streets here? My idea was okay; only in this world center can one collect information quickly enough to strike efficiently. Who wants to hear how I made those ten big ones?"

Little Giant gave Mathilde the menu. "Take some sashimi, that isn't just herring torn from the sea and dumped in salt like we do at home, but a complete gourmet dish of selected seafood. Syben and I had some yesterday."

"Fully recommended," Syben said.

"I'm glad you took us here," Mathilde said, "Mark only has time to grab hamburgers, and Van Putte lives on crackers and weak tea. Relax, Mark, and enjoy a good meal."

"I'll just take some fried rice," Mark said, "what that man over there is eating. That looks safe enough. Japanese cooking is too foreign for me. Do you want to know how I collected that ten thousand dollars? Another feat, eh? Eh? *Eh?*"

"Or have tempura," Little Giant said. "Vegetable fritters."

Syben pointed at the sideboard, "Or some of those sushi. Excellent as an appetizer."

A kimono-clad girl took the order, smiling and tittering. Mark frowned. "What is that girl tee-heeing about? I didn't say anything funny, did I? I mistrust those Easterners as much as their food. Why didn't we go for some fried potatoes and steak? For the last time, do you want to know how I am increasing our capital? I think you're just jealous of my intelligence and energy."

"Could be," Mathilde said, "because *my* attempt failed completely. I'm sorry, Mark. Please tell me what you did."

"You don't have to overact," Mark said. "You were there when I collected the smackeroos. I was addressing my brothers."

"Who are listening to you," Syben said.

"At Van Putte's office," Mark said, "'I met a gentleman who, later when Mathilde and I were having a quick lunch in one of Wall Street's side alleys, joined us at our table. He was talking about foreign exchange and intimated that the Swiss franc would be going up."

"I know what he looked like," Little Giant said. "He was black, dressed in a fur coat, and carried a cane with a communicating silver knob on top."

"No," Mark said, "he wore a blue three-piece suit and had white hair tucked over his ears."

"So you bought Swiss francs," Syben said, "and risked all again. Right?"

Mark inserted his chopsticks into his rice. The rice slid away between the polished wood. Mathilde held up her hand and arranged the chopsticks. "Do it this way. Hold the one between your thumb and middle finger and the other one like a pencil between your middle and index finger, like this, see?"

"Mark is clumsy," Little Giant said.

"And hold the bowl close to your mouth in order to decrease the distance."

"Yes," Mark said, and took a spoon. "Indeed, Syben, I went all out again. I had to buy traveler's checks because I didn't have an account with the bank. The girls who had to fill in the checks went crazy, and even crazier today because I returned all the checks again."

"And there was that much difference in the total dollar value?"

Mark pulled a newspaper from his side pocket and showed Syben a red-lined item. "Look for yourself, the Swiss franc shot up."

"I never," Little Giant said.

"You don't approve?"

"A ten-thousand-dollar profit is okay, but the franc could have gone down."

"You eat your raw fish," Mark said. "The franc went up, and not only because that Wall Street gentleman wanted it to. By the time you get up in the morning, I have read six newspapers. I knew the dollar was uncertain, and my suspicion was confirmed, just for a day, but that was all I needed."

"Congratulations," Little Giant said. "Can we leave now? I've seen New York. Those skyscrapers are no more than tottering, moldy ruins. We are spending three hundred dollars a day to be allowed to listen to gas bubbles in rusty tubes."

"No light without shadow," Mark said. "Walk down Fifth Avenue and see what American effort can do. The positive genies that created those lovely towers of glass now live in me, too. In just a few moments I've recouped our Tunisian losses. Our capital is back to its previous size, but my profitable energy is still flowing strongly. I would like to hear some feedback," Mark said.

"I'm eating right now," Little Giant said.

"Money is paper," Syben said. "Dad showed us that. I think we have enough by now."

"Money provides a safe feeling."

"What?" Little Giant asked. "In the way you're handling it? In order to make that hundred thousand, you risked ten times as much as we had, and if the franc's value had just dropped a little. . . . I don't even want to think about the risks you take. I'm tired of walking on the brink of damnation. Let's get the hell out of here, I say. Let's have some fun, I say. Let's rent a large limousine, buy six crates of beer, rent some clown suits and a set of drums. Just imagine, Mark, Arizona's desert, with cactuses the size of pine trees, Las Vegas, with stages filled with ladies as lovely as Mathilde but who have forgotten to get dressed. Cool champagne next to a swimming pool under New Mexico's tropical sky. A helicopter flight, and the Rocky Mountains beneath us. A ride in an antique streetcar up a hill in San Francisco. To follow the

coastal highway to Big Sur, to cross the ocean in a cruise ship
to Hawaii."

"Just give me a little more time," Mark said, "and we'll do
all that. And more. In America they always do more. I know
what you mean. Another beer, Syben?"

"No," Syben said. "And I have a feeling Little Giant is
right. The quicker we get out of this town the better. Maybe
there'll be some Van Puttes in California, but if we go broke
there, we will have at least seen something of the country."

"Broke," Mark said. "What a joke. Haven't I convinced
you yet that I'm on the right path?" He rubbed his belly.
"It's glowing inside here and when it glows, it means that I'm
making the right choices. Don't forget, I've been trained for
this type of commerce, and I can apply my intuition in a
suitable manner. Just let me go on for a little while. As soon
as I feel that it's time for a break, we'll leave."

"Pigskins?" Little Giant asked the next day at lunch.

"Yes," Mark said, "and the piglets haven't even been born
yet. The name of the game is *futures*. Pigskins are cheap right
now, but the experts expect much future demand, although
the hacks are despondent enough to get out of the market.
There has been some pig plague in Texas and another out-
burst in Louisiana, and those two states are the main suppliers. These days the futures can be picked up easily, but the
market is due to turn any moment."

"Did you buy them already?" Syben asked.

"Yes."

"Let's see them."

Mark held up his hand. "How can I show you air? I
already said that the pigs that will carry the skins aren't even
around yet."

"So show me the papers. Some bill of sale."

"There are no papers. Whatever I bought is in my name
now, and Van Putte knows. That's all I need."

"You bought them with a partial payment again?"

"Of course. You always have to go in for the whole hog if

you want to make a big profit. Pigs are around by the millions."

"You're pulling the devil by the tail," Little Giant said.

"I'm financing future wealth. By paying in now, I'm supplying the pig raisers with cash so that their sows may be fertilized and fodder can be bought."

"Bah," Little Giant said.

"I say, Mark," Syben said, "would you happen to be carrying any loose cash?"

"Yes, why?"

Syben put out his hand. "One thousand dollars please."

"What do you want with a thousand dollars?"

"Spend it," Syben said.

Little Giant put out his hand, too.

"Two thousand dollars? What's with you all of a sudden?"

"Give cash," Syben said, "we are your brothers. If you can invest it in pigs, you can invest it in us."

"I don't have that much on me."

Little Giant indicated Mark's mouth with his fork. "There are some green leaves hanging out of your maw; you're looking a little like a pig yourself. Don't be a skinflint, Mark. When the waves pushed you on a beach on Corsica, Syben helped you, too. Repay the favor."

Mark ate more lettuce.

"I do believe you should give it to them," Mathilde said. "We know that you're making money for us, too, but surely you can spare some of the capital."

"You want a thousand dollars, too?"

"The pig here has been making a mess," Little Giant said, "and I find it hard to put up with the stench. I'm going to my room. Are you coming Syben?"

Mathilde got up, too.

"I'm sorry," Mark said. "I'll bring you the money in a moment."

"Poor Mark," Mathilde said.

CHAPTER 15

"THE NAME is Goldstein," the man behind the monumental desk said. "What can I do for you?"

"Sobryne," Little Giant said. "I have a few stamp albums with me, and I'd like to show them to you."

The man got up, but his head stayed at the same level behind the desk. He walked around the desk and shook Little Giant's hand. He was a little smaller than his visitor. Little Giant laughed and begged his host's pardon.

"Do they often laugh about you, too?" Goldstein asked.

"Often," Little Giant said. "But I got used to it."

Goldstein pointed at an antique sculptured chair and sat down opposite Little Giant. He had a beard, too, but longer and more flowing than Little Giant's, and his sedate dark suit was either new or had been cleaned recently. A spotless, immaculately folded handkerchief protruded from his breast pocket, and a large pearl gleamed on his necktie. "I'll never get used to it; it is a curse to have to present oneself as a dwarf."

Little Giant accepted the offered cigar and struck a match. He gave Goldstein a light first. "You're no dwarf, and neither am I. We just happened to come out somewhat on the small side, but our size is quite acceptable. What a splendid office you have."

Goldstein smiled. "Do you think so? I try to exhibit good taste. Anyone can surround himself with beautiful things. I'm a collector; everything you see here is sixteenth-century oak. That sideboard originates in a British lord's castle. I only recently acquired the item."

"And the mirrors?"

"From Spain."

"And these chairs and the side table?"

"They're from Armenia; my father brought them when we emigrated to America."

"And you also collect stamps?"

Goldstein waved his hands in protest. "Please. Isn't my burden sufficiently heavy? If the stamps stuck to me, too, I wouldn't be able to feed my family."

Little Giant unzipped his bag. "Perhaps I'm wasting your time, but I would like to know what this collection is worth. My father collected stamps, but he died, and because I had to go to America anyway, I took his collection along. He only saved American stamps, and I thought that they would be more in demand over here than in Europe."

Goldstein adjusted his spectacles. "Your father passed away? I'm sorry to hear that. Did the two of you get along well?"

Little Giant placed two albums on the low table. "Yes, but to me he was different. He was a gentleman who lived on a high level beyond my reach."

"Are you being facetious?" Goldstein asked.

"I do not believe so."

"Was your father taller than you? Physically I mean?"

"That, too," Little Giant said.

Goldstein started with the second album and turned its pages quickly. The newer stamps didn't seem to interest him. He took more time when he looked through the first album with the older stamps.

"The last forty years are complete," Little Giant said.

"Maybe," Goldstein said, still turning pages, "I only really care for the older items; they sometimes have very attractive prices. Look here"—he pointed at a little gray portrait of Washington—"and this one, the Columbus dollar of 1893."

"What is that dollar stamp worth?"

"Whatever a fool thinks it's worth," Goldstein said. "Would you like some coffee?"

The coffee was served in a silver pot by an old lady. She poured it into porcelain cups. "Mother," Goldstein said, "this is Mr. Sobryne. He wants to know what the Columbus dollar stamp is worth."

"Hello, Mr. Sobryne," the old lady said, then clasped her hands and looked at the ceiling.

"You mean?" Little Giant asked.

"My mother means that a postage stamp is a small printed piece of paper," Goldstein said, "and has no real purpose, and therefore no true value. All you can do is stick it into an album and put the album away somewhere."

"But what about your sixteenth-century oak furniture?" Little Giant asked. "Didn't you pay for it from the profits made out of stamp dealing?"

Goldstein combed his beard lovingly with his hand. "Indeed I did, and perhaps it isn't right to make money out of the perverted greed of others. There was a time when I was almost guided into buying and selling arms. Postage stamps are a lesser evil."

"But they do have a purpose," the old lady said. "How would I ever have learned the names of American presidents if I hadn't studied stamps?"

Goldstein touched the red stamp. "And the fools did manage to fix a figure. In the catalog this one is priced at six hundred dollars."

"Which you will pay for it?"

"Maybe half?" Goldstein asked.

"And maybe that's too much," his mother said, "because Samuel has to get rid of it again. He's a dealer, Mr. Sobryne, and we live on his profits."

"Let's say the entire collection then, as it is here on the table?"

"Two thousand dollars," Goldstein said, "and only because I like you. I could auction the collection for you, in which case you might get more."

"Or less," Goldstein's mother said, "and then the commission has to be deducted. The next auction will be held in a few months' time."

"I thought it was worth more," Little Giant said.

Goldstein nodded. "I often hear that from my customers,

but the collection is not complete, you see. Let me show you." He turned the pages again. "Too many empty spots, which is a pity. I cannot sell it as a whole, and would have to split it into series. I'll surely sell them profitably, but it'll take much time."

"And trouble," the old lady said.

Little Giant counted the empty spaces. "Sixty-two missing stamps. Do they make that much difference?"

"All the difference."

"And if the collection was complete?"

"Then," Goldstein said, "I would beat the big drum and place an ad of a sixteenth of a page in *The New York Times*. We would be selling a great rarity. The United States complete. Step right up, step right up."

Mrs. Goldstein raised her arms above her head and stood on one foot. She was singing.

"An Armenian folk song," Goldstein said, "to celebrate holidays. They were rare, too."

"You have a beautiful voice," Little Giant said. He turned back to Mr. Goldstein. "And what will it cost to obtain the missing stamps?"

"If you are not in a hurry," Goldstein said, "and know how to handle a perforation measure and can learn to determine watermarks, and if you read the trade magazines and have the strength of character that controls the mind during auctions, you might go far on ten thousand dollars."

"Or more," Mrs. Goldstein said. "My son, unfortunately, is an optimist."

"And then what would my father's collection be worth?"

Goldstein turned another leaf. "Some of the present items will have to be replaced, like this one—rather a poor Garfield of six cents."

"Shent," Little Giant said, "the American *c* has a stroke through it you know. *We* just write cent, with an ordinary *c*. The 'sh' denotes the difference."

"Stroke? No, it misses part of the perforation. But that Garfield isn't expensive; I'll sell you a better one for eight dollars."

"A stroke through the shent, not through the stamp."

Goldstein wasn't listening. "And your fifty-shent Missis-sippi has been cut, by scissors probably, but that isn't a very costly one, either."

"Cent," Mrs. Goldstein said.

Little Giant replaced the album in his bag. He got up. "I thank you for your time and trouble."

"You aren't living here?" Goldstein asked.

"I live in Holland."

Goldstein caressed his beard. "Right. You'd be better off buying the missing stamps somewhere else. Outside the country of origin prices are usually lower, because the collecting rage aimed at stamps of a certain country increases as one gets closer to the source. Rather strange, really, because you would think that the exotic element would raise the price, but it seems that we prefer to realize our dreams at home. You have to go already?"

"I don't want to impose myself on you," Little Giant said.

Mrs. Goldstein smiled when she saw her son standing next to Little Giant. She sliced a cake and poured more coffee. "Samuel?"

"Yes, Mother."

"China."

"China it is," Goldstein said. "Mr. Sobryne, please sit down again. Eating while standing up is bad for the health. You are a traveler, but China is perhaps too far away for you. I do not want you to leave with empty hands. You do not wish to sell. Would you rather buy?"

"But I have some stamps already," Little Giant said.

Goldstein brought a box. "Now look at this."

Little Giant inserted his hand between the transparent envelopes.

"The albums are underneath," Goldstein said. "The collection is messy but sizable."

Little Giant opened an album. "China?"

"A long way off," Goldstein said, "and not much in demand here. A lot of work to sort this out, but you will learn much about an extraordinary civilization. What you have there is not uninteresting, if you have the time and inclination to get acquainted with the material."

"The expensive stamps are missing?"

"Not all of them."

"And what isn't there could be found?"

"Why not? You live in Europe and could check the large auctions. With what you already have here and what you can buy there, you could complete at least three collections."

"And then?"

"You could sell your merchandise with a considerable profit. There are very wealthy Chinese, Mr. Sobryne, and they're as bothered by inflation as we are. They must exchange banknotes that are continuously losing value for postage stamps that will be likely to be worth more as time passes by."

Little Giant held up a stamp. "Like this silly piece of paper displaying an ugly duck?"

Goldstein folded his hands. "Such is the faith, shared even by wise men in the East. Are we to take it upon ourselves to shake the faith of others?"

"What's in the box?" Syben asked.

"Chinese postage stamps," Little Giant said.

"You still have your thousand dollars?"

Little Giant pointed at the box. "All spent."

Syben put on his jacket. Little Giant took a step back without taking his eyes off his brother. "Wow. What's with you? A bum in mufti?"

Syben buttoned his silk shirt. "Mathilde likes dressing, and I thought I'd match her style."

Little Giant almost sat on his box. "Jeez, she might not even recognize you like that. Is this a new incarnation? You're trying to shake her?"

"Shock might help," Syben said. "Crack her defenses."

Little Giant opened his box and rummaged through its contents of torn plastic envelopes stuffed with stamps. "She's too sly for us."

Syben smoothed down his jacket. "For you and Mark. She recognizes your crude approach and rejects it."

Little Giant looked up. "Easy now. You want the same thing. She knows it." He shook his head. "Whatever your approach, she won't let you have it, either."

Syben combed his golden hair with short exact strokes. "Don't jump at low conclusions. She wants to be loved, and I want to provide that love, but she thinks I'm like you two. In order to point out the error, I'm now changing tactics."

"Maybe *that's* your problem," Little Giant said. "*High* conclusions. I never trusted your 'quest for truth.' Maybe you went to India to learn how to put a spell on beautiful women and to Africa to learn how to wipe out other lovers. You just want to be an all-over stud. What do you mean you want to *love* her?"

Syben knotted his new tie. "You're defining on the lower level. On my plane the activity is known as sharing spiritual growth, in another word: 'loving.' " He plopped down on Little Giant's bed. Little Giant raised his arms protectively. "Careful. The stamps."

"Sure." Syben picked up a stamp, lifting it carefully between his fingertips. He studied its image. "Three Chinese gents in frock coats and with slicked down hair, crowded into a medallion? What do you want them for?"

"For research," Little Giant said. "Find out what we have here. I'll spend all night if necessary." He flicked a nail against the box. "Got some catalogs, too. I'll check prices, maybe determine irregularities that may give the stamps more value."

Syben slid the stamp back into its envelope. "Good. You do that. A better project than trying to understand your betters."

"You just want to—"

Syben's hand covered Little Giant's mouth. "From where you are it has to look like that. Okay. Even translated down into your terms, I see no wrongdoing. What we have then is regular desires satisfied acceptably. We all indulge in hobbies. You play with postage stamps, Mark roots for cash, I romance my playmate of the year. We're all very happy."

"Not long-term," Little Giant said. "Mathilde doesn't want to rock the boat. We're in it, too."

Syben sighed. "So don't peek. Pretend it's bad weather." He smiled. "Help me with good thoughts?"

"Comrade," Little Giant said, "I'll be with you every millimeter of the way." He shook his fist in the Communist manner. "By the way, what has Mark planned for tonight?"

"Mark is going out tonight with Van Putte to a café where stockbrokers try to argue their clients into avoiding false steps. The pigskins have gone up just a little, and Mark intends to sell. Now he's enthusiastic about cocoa beans."

"Futures again?"

"Yes," Syben said, "and the bushes that are to grow those beans are still trying to push themselves up in between the weeds."

Little Giant jumped off the bed and stood in front of Syben. "We have to kidnap him. Let me rent a car tomorrow and drive it up front. You knock Mark down and throw him in the rear. The sooner we get out of here, the better."

"I'll first have to get rid of my obsession."

Little Giant emptied out his envelopes on the bed. The door slammed by Syben caused a draft, and the stamps fluttered about the room. Little Giant sighed, waited for the stamps to settle, knelt, and began to pick them up.

CHAPTER 16

"How sweet of you," Mathilde said, and slowly lowered her body into an easy chair upholstered with mauve velvet. "Where are we now?"

"Our hotel manager says it is the most elegant nightclub in New York City. There'll be music a little later. We can have a drink while we wait and eat something, perhaps. Would you care for caviar?"

"Yes," Mathilde said. "Caviar. Please. I really don't like it because it is fish sperm or eggs or something, but I managed to develop a taste for it so as not to disappoint your father. There were evenings when he put on his very best clothes and would watch me while I dressed. I had to wear my pearls, and he would fluff my hair. We would go to a concert or to the theater and for an elegant supper afterward. It never took too long because he tired quickly."

"I'm younger," Syben said.

"And more handsome. The way you look now, you are the exalted dream of an ecstatic schoolgirl." She grinned.

"Don't laugh at me," Syben said, "I'm doing my best."

She touched his hand. "I laugh because I'm happy, and something occurred to me. A long time ago, when I was very little, my own father used to take me to the zoo on Sunday mornings. It was in the summer, and there would be music from the bandstand. It was like it is now. I would sit on a lovely chair and my father would say, 'There'll be music a little later.' "

If the beginning is good, Syben thought, chances improve

that the end will be likewise. He ordered champagne cock-
tails and caviar.

"Are you going to wear that lovely suit all the time now?"
Mathilde asked.

"Would you like me to?"

"You look a little like Mark now."

That's not good, Syben thought.

"No," Mathilde said. "I am not expressing myself well.
You look like what Mark should look like."

That's better, Syben thought.

Mathilde arranged the folds in her skirt. She had, after
allowing the chair to embrace her, sat up again while taking
care that her legs, properly crossed, were displayed to maxi-
mum advantage. Her thighs, though covered by the skirt,
were clearly visible in outline. So was her bosom, tightly
filling the V-cut of her blouse and moving majestically as she
breathed. Her fresh skin gleamed like the pearls splendidly
arrayed around her neck, and their combined ivory tinge set
off deep red shades on her mouth and hair.

Syben looked into Mathilde's eyes. How can I define their
expression? Syben thought. As sleepy? No, that's a loutish
definition, although it's true that her eyes never merge completely with the outside world. Is she looking inside, so that
she can live in her thoughts, and feel secure within the
frontiers of her dreams? That isn't quite true, either, because
she does participate in the flow of life around her. Or is she
looking sexy in a civilized manner? Let's keep it at that.

He toasted her. "Do you think that Mark and I look alike?"

A slight vibration moved Mathilde's nose and touched the
corners of her mouth. "Mark deals in pigs."

"He deals in money," Syben said. "And the pigs are over
and done with already; now he's stuck in cocoa."

Mathilde accepted a light. "I never quite understood what
money is, not even when I had it myself. Money isn't real,
but it's always in everything, for without it daily life comes
to an end. The evening before I met your father, I was sitting
in a rented room and ate jam from a jar with my fingers. The
jam was moldy, and so was the wallpaper in the room."

Syben watched four tall black men climb onto the stage. "How did that come about?"

"I had run away from my husband. My husband was possessed by money; that's why I took nothing with me, because I wanted a complete separation. He was a promoter of illegal migrant labor."

"I know the trade. It's run by entrepreneurs who keep going bankrupt and getting richer."

"He drove a Cadillac that was too large to park, so he let me drive and yelled at me when I couldn't find a place. He would buy me anything, but usually I didn't like his gifts, and he'd get terribly angry."

"A bounder," Syben said sympathetically. Mathilde laughed.

"The description fits. He also liked watching porno movies on the video, and I had to select them, but now he isn't watching them anymore."

"He's blind?"

"He's dead." Mathilde's hand stiffened. "He left via a beach chair on the French coast with five bullets in his chest, and is now taking his part in hellish scenes."

"But you weren't involved in that, were you?"

"No, one of his colleagues helped him along. I was with your father in Kralingen."

"He left you his money?"

"His money was gone. I'm a poor widow."

The cynical intonation of her voice was taken over by the combo. A flute blew pure round notes, floating on swelling chords from the piano. The bass groaned sadly, but the piano player tried to break through the depression.

He had seen Mathilde and tuned into her mood. Mathilde smiled again. The music became less melancholy and even aggressive, because the drummer understood what inspired the piano player and began to hit the side of his snare drum lightly, to impose a line that could uphold the piano's flirtation. The flute stopped its efforts to dominate the melody and supported the drumming.

Watching the black hand plucking dissonance from the

piano keys, Syben stretched his back. "Would you like to dance?"

"In a minute," Mathilde said, "when there are some more people. Life starts late here. Could I have another drink?"

A young woman slid close, away, and back again, carrying the cocktail glasses in her hand.

"How cozy," Mathilde said. "They probably never heard of trays in this place. Is that woman just to serve drinks, or are there bedrooms available upstairs?"

"I don't think there are any bedrooms," Syben said.

"I'm sorry. I did sound a little annoyed, didn't I? But that girl touched you; her thigh pressed against your leg. And why did she call you General Custer?"

"She made a joke," Syben said. "General Custer was a famous Indian fighter, and I believe that he was tall and wore his hair in a ponytail."

"I think that girl is too forward," Mathilde said. "Perhaps I should complain to the management."

Syben caressed her hand. "Your beauty cannot be compared to the girl's appearance. Comparison between the two of you serves no purpose."

"Girl? That woman is the same age I am."

Syben glanced at the waitress. "It's about time that I ordered spectacles. Now, shall we dance?"

The piano player veered upright when he saw Mathilde approach the dance floor. He started a fast riff. The drummer followed as the bass player shook his wrists and attacked his strings violently.

Mathilde's close, vibrating body encouraged Syben to become one with the subtly mesmerizing melody in which the combo was finding itself. Syben's doubt, which sometimes cut through his better moments, faded away, and the excitement of his liberation caused him to lift his legs and stretch his arms. That he did so in a responsible and artistic manner was proved by the emptying of the dance floor and the well-mannered applause offered by the other guests.

"Syben," Mathilde said, "That was very nice. I wasn't

self-conscious, and I didn't overreact. You are a splendid dancer."

"I need more to drink," Syben said.

She nodded. "But the next cocktail will be my last tonight."

"And afterward we will go to that Japanese restaurant. You did like the food there, didn't you?"

"Yes," Mathilde said, "but I won't have too much."

There was no wind outside the club, and no mad persons to harass the pair. The cab was a brand-new vehicle and the driver a kindly old man who got out when he saw Mathilde and opened the door for her. The moon shone on Fifth Avenue and dispensed a calm and penetrating light that flooded glass towers reaching for a sky dotted with sparkling stars.

Syben felt caught in his self-invoked magic, whose grandeur impressed him pleasantly. He had become an unreal hero of the screen, in a decor that no earthly producer could have imagined. And next to him, in the taxi gliding through traffic lights that turned green as it approached, sat a fairy-tale Mathilde, accompanying him gently and submissively during this temporary adventure.

The Japanese restaurant also fit in with the heavenly escapade, and the favored couple enjoyed the performance of dainty young ladies tripping about in decorative kimonos; intricate spots of color against simple pine paneling. The attractively arranged dishes pleased their eyes, and the warm white wine their palates. It couldn't last forever.

"Home," Syben said.

They walked to the nearby hotel along the almost-empty streets. Here and there human shadows moved through the surrealist streetscape.

"Look," Mathilde said.

Mathilde saw an elderly gentleman entering a splendid antique car.

Syben watched the car smoothly join the sparse traffic. "Extraordinary."

"Didn't he look just like your father?"

"He did own that type of Packard," Syben said, "until a few years ago, when he stopped driving."

Mathilde stood in the open door, with the dark room behind her. The corridor light shone softly on her face and body and her head tilted a little backward.

Syben kissed her gently. "Sleep well."

Mathilde's soft arms closed around his neck as she stepped back.

CHAPTER 17

"NOT AGAIN," Little Giant said, and looked at the stamps fluttering away from his bed, night table, and desk. Mathilde stood in front of him and held her hand on her mouth. "What did I do?"

"You caused a draft," Little Giant said, "and now I can start all over again. Syben did it this morning when he came in, and once more when he left. But I get better every time at sorting them out."

Mathilde knelt down. "Shall I help you?"

Together they replaced Little Giant's stock in the box.

Little Giant had just showered and had wrapped himself in a towel. He smelled fragrantly of soap. The curls of his beard fitted airily into each other, and his pink ears stuck out from his drying hair. He sat on his bed, his legs folded into each other. "Would you like some coffee? They have just brought it. Nice and fresh."

"There's only one cup."

"After you," Little Giant said. "There is plenty in the carafe."

Mathilde sat next to Little Giant on the bed. She was wearing tight slacks with the zipper on the side. Little Giant unzipped the slacks.

"Don't do that, Little Giant."

"Why shouldn't I?" Little Giant asked. "That is the pleasure of living in a hotel. One is lifted out of one's normal routine and granted the possibility of predicting the extraordinary. Don't you prefer the extraordinary to the normal routine?" He undid the snap above the zipper. "If you get up now, your pants will come off by themselves, I won't be doing anything, so you can't hold that against me."

Mathilde got up.

Little Giant jumped off the bed and ran to the door. He turned the key and inserted the chain. "If I had done this earlier, my stamps wouldn't have blown away, but you wouldn't have been able to come in, either."

"In which case you would have prevented two calamities. Do try and behave, Little Giant."

Little Giant's hands slid along her blouse and pushed the buttons through the buttonholes. "Please sit down again; my arms are too short."

"I can keep standing and take my shoes off."

Little Giant considered the choice. "No."

Mathilde waited patiently.

"But if you kept your shoes on, your towering height could add to the excitement."

"But then you can't reach too well."

"I can reach," Little Giant said. "Stand in front of the bed, then I'll get on the bed, which makes me taller than you are."

I don't know who or what I should thank for this, Little Giant thought, but this is hardly the moment for questioning. He jumped off the bed, opened up the sheets and conducted Mathilde to her fated destination.

Now let's not rush, Little Giant said to himself; a good lover knows how to contain himself and takes his time, even if he's both upset and astounded by the unexpected change of luck, so that his heart is palpitating and his normal breathing interrupted.

Little Giant took his time, and more than an hour had passed when Mathilde pulled the door of her own room closed behind her.

Mark was downstairs, talking to Van Putte. Syben observed.

"So you think I should unload?" Mark asked. "But those crazy beans will be going up again. Why should I get off the train when the train is still moving?"

"I think that all this talk about a possible civil war in

Ghana is exaggerated," Van Putte said, "and even if there is some unrest out there, nothing will happen to raise the price of cocoa beans." He waved a leaflet in Mark's face. "Mark, listen to good advice. This expert paper deals with cocoa and contains recent figures on the producing countries. Ghana only supplies a small share of the world's production, so what does it matter if the crop isn't harvested this year? Nigeria is expecting a surplus, and the South Americans are doing better every year; there may be more cocoa available than ever before."

"And what about your own information? Your computerized data that represent the actual exact situation? Wasn't the price up two points yesterday?"

"A little panic," Van Putte said, "like we've just had in cotton. Some little worm could have been feasting on the weed, but this morning cotton opened ten points lower. Overall images are far too complex to gauge correctly. All the computer can do is indicate present and past values."

Mark killed his cigarette with a nicotine-smudged finger. He had been biting his nails. "So I've got to sell?"

"I would think so. Cocoa is no longer of interest, and the other futures are beyond my comprehension. If I were you, I would take my loss and wait quietly until the situation clarifies again. There is never any real need to speculate. What could keep forcing you to renew your effort continuously?"

"A loss?" Syben asked.

"A small loss," Van Putte said. "Cocoa is going down, and whenever it veers up, the gain is only temporary. Mark still has some space now, but if the value of the futures keeps dropping, he will be with his back to the wall, a position I do not recommend to any of my clients."

"There are the morning papers," Mark said, and rushed to the news desk in the hall.

"Do you hold any cocoa futures yourself?" Syben asked.

Van Putte frowned. "I don't hold anything except the safest of the safe, and then widely spread and in small quantities. My adventures are all in the past. I lost my shirt twice, and once even filed for bankruptcy. That the bankruptcy wasn't confirmed was because my creditors thought that I would gamble my way out again. I did but swore that I would never repeat the experience."

"I thought you were rich."

"What is rich?"

"To be rich," Syben said, "means that one can live decently and continue to do so for the rest of ones' life without any exertion."

"Then I'm not rich. I buy more food in a week than a citizen of Haiti in a year, but my house isn't worth more than the mortgage, and of my three cars, two need urgent repairs. My income is unsteady and goes down whenever I don't watch it."

"And your only income consists of your commissions?"

Van Putte looked over his shoulder. "Just look at Mark tearing the papers apart. I can't stand the sight." He got up. "Sure, I live on my commissions, and my clients keep coming back to me because they know I won't allow them to go broke. If Mark keeps going the way he is, he will no longer be my client."

"Where is Van Putte?" Mark asked.

"He had to go back to his office, but asked if you would phone him in an hour."

"To tell him that I'll sell my beans, I suppose." Mark dropped into a chair. He rubbed his bulging belly. "I still have a safe feeling. Those pigskins went down as well, but recovered again the next day. I absolutely refuse to take another loss."

Syben spoke to Mathilde, and they both then spoke to Little Giant.

"No," Little Giant said, "Mark isn't quite right in the head now. With the insane you have to wait until the attack is over. Besides, I don't mind if he falls flat on his face for a change. The way he is behaving now is hard to put up with."

"The satisfaction," Syben said, "although not unwelcome, might be rather costly."

*   *   *

"I'll see what I can do for you," Syben said to Mathilde in the corridor.

"It isn't just for me," Mathilde said. "If you can talk Mark into selling, you will strengthen our joint position."

Syben caressed Mathilde's arm. She pushed his hand away and said, "Last night was last night. I would prefer that you'd forget my weak moment."

"I adore you."

"The feeling will pass."

"I'll do anything for you."

"Then talk to Mark. I want to leave this place."

"Phone Van Putte," Syben said to Mark.

"Don't threaten me. Phone him or what?"

"Or nothing," Syben said. "I'm only trying to help you."

"In proving that I don't even know anything about my own field?"

A bellboy carried a large slate through the lobby. The name "Sobryne" had been chalked on the slate. The boy hit a bell.

Syben walked to the boy. "Yes?"

"You're wanted on the telephone, sir."

"It's for you," Syben said to Mark. "A voice from the grave."

He waited until Mark came back. "Well?"

"The bastard sold my cocoa beans."

"Right."

'Right," Mark repeated tremulously. "Don't you understand what I'm saying? He could only sell them without my consent if they dropped to my minimum. I had put in two hundred thousand, and now my loss equals two hundred thousand. Van Putte couldn't hold them any longer unless I paid in more, and he knows that I can't."

"Is that so?" Syben said.

"And he calls himself my friend," Mark said. "Tomorrow those beans will be up again." He lit a filter cigarette on the wrong side. Syben pulled the cigarette out of Mark's mouth, broke off the burning filter, and reinserted it between Mark's lips. He flicked his lighter. "Did you pay the hotel bill?"

"No."

"Do you have enough money in your credit card?"

"No."

"So where did you get the two thousand dollars that you gave to Little Giant and me?"

"Some of the profit on the Swiss francs that I kept back."

"I thought you had made more."

"I was bragging some," Mark said, "and most of what I made I put in again. It doesn't matter anymore. If I had made more, I would have put it into cocoa, too."

"I still have a few hundred dollars," Syben said. "It was an expensive evening, and I also bought a suit."

"And Little Giant?"

"He invested in stamps."

Mark groaned.

"Little Giant and I still have our own share of the inheritance; we can have some of it sent in."

"On a Friday? The weekend has already started."

"Dinnertime," Syben said. "You can choose the restaurant. The universe is still turning."

"Have you calculated how far your credit card will take us?" Little Giant asked.

"I'm short two thousand dollars."

"There'll be an airplane to Amsterdam tomorrow morning," Mathilde said. "Let's leave as soon as possible and have some peace in Mark's apartment. That won't cost three hundred dollars a day, and I can cook cheaply."

"But how do we pay the hotel?" Mark asked. "Or would you rather leave the luggage and clear out in silence? That isn't quite my style."

"Sir is a nobleman," Little Giant said, "but only a little while ago Sir was smuggling drugs, and since then he has been dealing in rather expensive air."

Mark looked at his plate, Syben looked at the ceiling, and Mathilde stared over Little Giant's head.

"I do beg your pardon," Little Giant said. "I had forgotten that traffic in hashish is legal in Tunisia and that we would deliver outside territorial waters. I do not wish to embezzle a hotel, either. Neither do I want to tease my brother. I got angry for a minute because I'm not sufficiently advanced to handle so much misfortune all at once. Now will you look at me again?"

He was looked at.

"Thank you," Little Giant said. "I met a friend here who's about my size and whose name is Goldstein. He offered me two thousand dollars for Dad's incomplete American stamp collection. I'll see him in the morning."

Syben patted Little Giant on his shoulder, Mark shook his hand, and Mathilde kissed his cheek.

ROTTERDAM
AGAIN

CHAPTER 18

THE BROTHERS were working.

"Isn't this nice?" Mathilde asked. "I'll be helping you in a minute, but now we'll have a coffee break and some home-made cookies. Oh, I really like Little Giant's idea. This is much more fun than New York, because out there only Mark could do something, but now we're in it all together."

"Don't make a draft," Mark said, and protected with his arm the stamps that he'd been selecting at his desk. "I do believe that I finally have a complete series of little dragons."

Syben knelt in front of a low coffee table. "Don't put it here Mathilde, because I've got something together, too—postage-due stamps from the northeastern provinces, or are they some kind of tax seals? I keep forgetting."

"Not here," Little Giant said, "or it'll be the end of my series of double carps." Little Giant sat at the dining table, on which a magnifying light had been installed. There were albums on the table. A pair of tweezers glistened in his gesturing hand.

"So where?" Mathilde asked.

"On the floor."

Mathilde placed the coffee tray on the carpet. She clapped her hands. "Break. Yes," Mathilde said, "I never knew what it was like to live with a family. This is pleasant. Tonight I'll make goulash and rice because you all like that."

Mark nibbled a cookie. "But you do have a brother, that gentleman in St. Tropez."

"My parents were divorced, and my brother was usually with my father."

"And you were with your mother?"

"No," Mathilde said, "my mother was away. I lived in a boarding school and was being trained to be a lady."

"That's why you're so sexy," Mark said. "Boarding school girls have an elevated style. They're also sneaky, but when they grow up the affliction changes into refinement."

Mathilde drank her coffee.

"Don't mind him," Little Giant said, "even if he is right. Mark can never be nice for long. Regrets don't last. We may be thankful that he managed to keep his big mouth shut for a week."

"Listen here," Mark said, "I know I did it all wrong, but I won't suffer forever. A misanthrope will be hard to handle by his associates, and you did admit that you couldn't handle this business alone. If I have to help, I should be allowed to behave normally."

Syben took a cookie, too. "And that he teases Mathilde is very understandable." He looked at Mathilde. "You shouldn't blame his nastiness. You are a perfect symbol, a fantasy shaped out of living flesh, an ostentatious open emptiness that we want to fill with our lower lusts; you are . . ."

"Sit down, Mathilde," Little Giant said, "and finish your coffee."

Mathilde stamped her foot. "I am not sitting down. I'm going to pack my suitcase!"

Little Giant pulled her skirt. "Sit down, I say. If you leave, we will be going with you. You have been chained to us."

"You are ripping my skirt."

Little Giant looked mean. "And your blouse, and your underwear. Heh heh heh."

"And once we've ripped it all off, we will be raping you cruelly," Mark said.

"Yes," Syben said, laughing. "Mhree mhree."

Mathilde sat down. She pushed against Syben's shoulder. "Stop grinning so vulgarly. You're usually so calm and polite. Why have you suddenly become degenerate?"

"Because I saw it all happening," Syben said. "Mhree mhree. You in convulsions on the floor and we . . ."

"And why am I chained? I'm a free woman. Nobody can stop me from leaving."

Little Giant put down his cup. "You have been chained by a lost million." He rattled his cup on the saucer. "We haven't been discussing that lately, but it isn't something to forget easily. One of us is a despicable thief hiding behind a polite mask. Every time I realize that fact, it drives me crazy." He belched softly. "Bah."

"Bah what?"

"Stomach acid," Little Giant said. He belched again. "I don't understand you. Look at you. All those smooth faces. Dad leaves us his capital, earned diligently, saved solidly, and before you can count the coins, half of them are gone. Does anyone ever mention the discrepancy?" He belched again, so loudly that he excused himself. "Nobody says a word. Everybody enjoys himself on camels, bathes in blue seas, hangs out in New York alleys, spends whatever is left, but do you ever hear anyone question where, goddammit, an entire million blew to? Which, goddammit, I was sleeping next to? In my innocence? Do you hear, goddamn . . ."

"Don't curse," Mathilde said.

"Easy now, Little Giant," Mark said.

"I don't really want to mind your business," Syben said, "but couldn't it perhaps be that you, in your innocence, almost suffocated in genever vapors, did manage to wake up at night, and after some shallow thought, accidentally as it were, slipped into our joint—I say joint—inheritance?"

"That's the bloody limit," Little Giant shouted. "I, who represent kindness itself, modesty itself, I, who immediately granted Mathilde her quarter share that wasn't even legal, that was only mentioned by Dad on the tape, while he was perhaps dying already and therefore unaware of his sentimental but maybe not quite acceptable and therefore possibly wrong recommendation. I, who was thrown on a camel and . . ."

"That was your own desire,' Syben said. "Who prattled on

about camels before we ever saw one? And who fouled the poor animal and insulted its character in such a way that the poor thing had to leak all over whose clothes to make matters right again and . . ."

"That'll be enough," Mark said.

"Why?" Little Giant asked. "Therapeutically this exchange of words could be very useful, to allow hidden agression to find a way out. . . ."

"This is not an encounter group," Mark said. "We are making money here. Now, how were we going to make money again, Little Giant?"

"I'll explain again," Little Giant said. "My friend Goldstein said that his box contained almost complete Chinese stamp collections, and he was right, because we have almost filled several albums already. I paid a thousand dollars for the lot, and according to the catalog we now have a collection that's worth almost ten thousand dollars. But nobody, according to my friend Goldstein, will ever pay the catalog value, not even rich Chinese in Hong Kong who want to safeguard their money from inflation. And what's more, that type of rich Chinese want complete collections to pull out of their safe every now and then to show to jealous acquaintances."

"So what is missing in our albums?" Mark asked.

"The most expensive stamps," Little Giant said. "And rightly so, because Goldstein sold me that box, and he isn't crazy. So we will have to find the expensive items some-where, and Goldstein says we have to find them here, be-cause here people don't know much about Chinese stamps."

"And the next move?" Syben asked.

Little Giant bowed in Mark's direction. "Brother Mark, who has a Ph.D. in the administration of wealth, and who also happens to be equipped with an oversized brain, even if he does slip up now and then, has thought of the next move. We will advertise."

"Which necessitates incorporating a business."

"Which we have done meanwhile. Sobryne & Company. The nameplate arrived today and has already been screwed to the front door."

"Pull in your lower lip, Mathilde," Syben said. "When you pout, you destroy the image I have of you."

"I'm sorry," Mathilde said, "I didn't know I was pouting."

"Why should that lower lip be withdrawn?" Little Giant asked. "I'd rather she pushed it out; she looks more 'kissy' that way."

"If the gentlemen could agree on how they would like me to express myself," Mathilde said.

"How much money would you invest before we go to Hong Kong?" Mark asked.

"A lot," Little Giant said. "A complete Chinese collection includes the Old Empire, the Republic, Communist China, Taiwan, and the provinces, and the cities—because Shanghai, for instance, issued its own stamps for several years—and all the overprints and the special issues dating from the Japanese occupation. That would come to about twenty-five thousand dollars. The trick is to build up as many complete collections as possible. At an auction, because other possibilities won't really be available to us out there, they might realize some twelve thousand dollars each. So far we have only invested a thousand. I had thought to spend some five thousand on advertising in several well-known newspapers, and another ten or fifteen for traveling expenses, and the rest on buying."

"Your share is about two hundred thousand guilders, which is about half in dollars," Syben said. "You can spend that much."

"I do hope you'll pull it off," Mathilde said.

"Well," Mark said, "that's what we thought when we were into hashish, and again in New York. But once we should be successful. That is the law of large numbers."

Syben covered his eyes with one hand. "The law of large numbers." He pressed his other hand on his eyes as well. "The law of one, two, *three* you mean."

"So, let's not do it," Mark said. "That's all right with me. We still have four hundred thousand guilders, which we can split into a hundred thousand each. We say good-bye to each other, and that'll be the end of that."

Little Giant tried to belch again. "We have to stay together, and this stamp business will make that possible for a while. It can also make us rich. It made Goldstein very wealthy."

"How do you know?"

"Because his furniture is sixteenth-century oak." Little Giant rolled backward over his head and landed on his legs. "Mark, I'm not sure of anything." He thumped his belly. "But I do have a safe feeling. We'll make it this time."

"That's what I thought in America, and Mathilde in Tunisia."

"So, are we going to set up the ads?" Mathilde asked.

CHAPTER 19

"No ma'am. I can't quite make out on that," Little Giant said.

The fat lady wore a hat and sat on the edge of her seat. She looked angrily at Little Giant.

"You do," Little Giant agreed, "have quite a lot of stamps here, but most of them are new. All recent issues, as you can see for yourself."

"My husband saved them," the lady said. "He was with the merchant marine, going to the East, but now he's dead."

143

"I'll give you a thousand guilders for the lot," Little Giant said.

The lady leaned on her umbrella.

"Yes?" Little Giant asked.

"You won't give me any more?"

"No, otherwise I won't quite make out on it."

"Give here, those thousand guilders," the lady said.

"No," Syben said, "I can't quite make out on that."

"Six hundred guilders for a shoe box full of stamps?" the young man in the leather jacket asked. "But that can't be enough. Do you know anything about stamps?"

"What is knowledge?" Syben asked. "I know what they're worth to me, and they're not for me. I have to sell them again."

"Some of them are quite beautiful, with strange animals sniffing each other's rear ends. Look at the ornamentation."

"I did, just now," Syben said, "and the catalog value will be more than what I'm offering, but nobody ever pays the catalog value."

"So, why is there a catalog value?" the young man asked.

"Somebody will always come up with prices," Syben said. "But nobody else will quite believe what he says."

The young man pulled the box toward him.

"Six hundred guilders," Syben said. He produced his wallet.

The young man turned at the door, put out his hand, and walked back to Syben's desk.

"There you are," Syben said. "With my thanks."

"No," Mark said, "I can't quite make out on that."

"Sir," the gentleman in the hundred-percent-cotton suit said, "what you are looking at now is unique. All Chinese postage-due stamps complete."

"They aren't worth much. Here is the catalog; why don't you check the prices?"

"I know the prices," the gentleman said. "The overprints are quite expensive, especially the 1912 issues."

"They are, but they seem to be missing."

The gentleman got up and turned pages in an album. "Missing, are they?" He pointed accusingly. "Right in front of your nose. Overprinted in red."

"You're right," Mark said, "but just red print isn't enough in this case. I trust you read some Chinese. What it says on your stamps is insufficient. There are some characters missing."

The gentleman sat down again. "So what are you looking for? What I'm offering you is a lovely collection." He jumped up again. "Like here, for instance, this Sun Yat-sen series alone is worth three hundred."

Mark held up a finger. "Aren't you exaggerating a little? Two hundred is closer and that is the *catalog* value; you know that nobody ever pays that."

"Now listen here," the gentleman said, "check the first page of the first album that I gave you. The ten-cent overprint on twelve-cent orange. Is that stamp worth two hundred and fifty guilders or not?"

"Just a minute," Mark said. "You are thinking of *light* orange. But what I see here is dark orange and not quite worth ten guilders."

"Ah," the gentleman said.

"Yes," Mark said.

"I must have made a mistake," the gentleman said, "I'm color-blind, you know."

"You are?"

"I am, but you still can't deny that I'm offering you interesting merchandise."

"Most interesting," Mark said, "and that's why I offered you three thousand guilders."

"Right," the gentleman said. "Three thousand guilders for the first album, and I'll be taking the rest home again."

"Not right," Mark said. "Three thousand for all three albums and the stock book with the assorted doubles."

"You're ripping me off."

Mark put down three thousand-guilder notes.

The gentleman hesitated.

Mark picked up the notes again.

"Don't touch," the gentleman said, "because they're mine."

*   *   *

"Hello," Mathilde said to the boy wearing sneakers.

"Hello. Are you buying Chinese stamps?"

"I'm not," Mathilde said, "but the gentlemen in the other rooms will buy them. Why don't you sit down for a moment?"

"I have to go," the boy said after a few minutes. "I've got to play softball."

"Do you have the stamps in your bag?"

"Would you like to see them?"

"What beautiful stamps," Mathilde said.

"There is an unbroken sheet," the boy said, "with airplanes all over. The airplanes are flying across the Chinese wall."

"But they're messed up a little, aren't they? Look at all these little squiggles."

"They don't matter much," the boy said. "Some of them should have squiggles. Many Dutch stamps have them, too, like those of Queen Wilhelmina when she was a little girl. They're called over-prints."

"I do like your stamps. How much do you want for them?"

"A hundred guilders." The boy's voice suddenly squeaked.

Mathilde studied the stamps. "They're just like Eastern rugs, so pretty; why don't you keep them?"

"I only collect the Netherlands, ma'am. China is no fun. If I want to show Chinese stamps, everybody walks away."

The telephone rang. "Excuse me," Mathilde said. "Yes?"

"I got to play softball," the boy said.

"Mr. Kulve?" Mathilde asked. "Are you coming all the way from the North? Sure, we'll be here, Mr. Kulve, and you can visit us until seven o'clock. Eight o'clock, you say, and you have some Chou En-lai with the lovely girls? Okay, we'll wait for you."

"Wherever did you get these stamps?" Mathilde asked.

The boy shrugged. "I traded them at school for some King Willem the Third, with a boy from another school. I'll sell them for eighty guilders."

Mathilde sighed, "We're so busy today. Can't you really wait for a few more minutes?"

"I got to play softball."

"Here you are," Mathilde said. "Eighty guilders to you."

"I'm glad we're almost done," Mark said. "Today is the last day; I'm going crazy with all these stamps. They keep on carrying in Chiang Kai-chek mausoleums and Mao Tse-tung holding up his red book."

"And dancing children," Syben said.

"And tractors in corn fields," Little Giant said, "and conquered Tibetans, and Korean veterans visiting their mothers, and sporty ladies teaching class."

"And whatever you offer is always too little," Mark said.

"It *is* always too little," Syben said.

"A hundred and fifty thousand guilders isn't enough?" Little Giant asked.

"And those horrible little boys," Mathilde said. "They kept hanging around me, and everything costs a hundred guilders. I took care of a few today. You were all too busy, and they never wanted to wait."

"That's it," Mark said. "I won't do any more. How many collections do we have now?"

"Twenty," Little Giant said, "and all the boxes with assorted stamps."

"And you think you can sell that for half a million?" Syben asked.

"Yes," Little Giant said squeakily.

The bell rang.

"Kulve," the gentleman said. "I've come all the way from the North. Do you want to buy my stamps?"

"We have so many stamps already," Little Giant said, "but do sit down please."

"You said," Mr. Kulve said, "that you'd buy anything as long as it was Chinese. For cash. I came all the way from the North."

Mr. Kulve left with two thousand guilders.

"What happened to all the horseplay?" Syben asked. He got up, bent his knees, and said in Little Giant's voice, "I can't quite make out on that, Mr. Kulve."

"You just gave that man what he wanted," Mark said, "and he only had Communist issues, the cheapest of them all, according to the catalog."

Little Giant pushed Mr. Kulve's album away. "Some of them are unused and worth money, like these, for instance, with the little boys doing gymnastics."

"Little Giant was tired," Mathilde said.

The bell rang.

A lady came in.

"Let's see what you have, ma'am," Mark said, "but you've really come too late."

The lady was Chinese, and spoke nothing else.

Syben gestured invitingly.

The lady emptied a transparent envelope.

"Those are Korean stamps," Little Giant said.

"How did you know?" Mathilde asked when the lady had gone.

"Because they showed white/black discs in the frames, expressing Yin and Yang, male and female, symbolizing the creation together."

"Female is white?" Mathilde asked.

"Black."

"But with a small white dot in the middle," Syben said.

"So I can't be bad all through," Mathilde said.

"Who says that female is bad?" Syben asked. "Black is a color of sultry, warm mud that is fertilized by the clear light."

"*Mud?*" Mathilde asked.

The bell rang.

Mark checked his watch. "It's after nine; we have no further appointments."

Little Giant switched off the lights. Syben forced his handkerchief into the bell. Together they stumbled through the corridor.

"Is that you?" Mark asked.

Mathilde slapped his hand away.

"Come with me," Mark whispered.

"No," Mathilde said in a loud voice.

"Leave her in peace," Little Giant and Syben said.

Mathilde lay in bed and felt her breathing slowing down.

"Hello?" asked old Mr. Sobryne.

"It's you," Mathilde said. "How nice. I do miss you, you know."

Old Mr. Sobryne stood in front of her in a velvet dressing gown tied with a cord ending in tassels. He had just come out of the bathroom and was smoking a small cigar.

"I loved you the most like that," Mathilde said, "because whenever you relaxed, you looked so kind and wise. I was very happy with you. Do you know that, True Gentleman from the Past?"

Old Mr. Sobryne looked guilty.

"And you were always so modest and polite."

Old Mr. Sobryne smiled sheepishly.

"But what you've pushed us into now rather makes me doubt those qualities," Mathilde said. "That hashish was a silly business, and I would never have gotten into that mess if you hadn't said at the time that you admired my brother so, and that you had wanted to live like him, busy with risky adventures, marauding from a picturesque villa on the Riviera."

Old Mr. Sobryne gestured apologetically.

"And that gambling in New York was pure lunacy, and I should have stopped Mark, but you said that you were sorry that you had never taken the slightest risk."

Old Mr. Sobryne blew a smoke ring. Mathilde laughed. "You could never quite do that. So, you can do it now?"

Old Mr. Sobryne looked proud.

"You are a dear," Mathilde said. "But now, what about these stamps? You had a pleasant hobby, but Little Giant is only interested in hard cash. Are you sure that is right?"

Old Mr. Sobryne grinned.

The heavenly light that surrounded Sobryne's apparition faded. Mathilde woke up. A streetlight shining softly through tulle curtains lit up the flowers on Mark's guest room wallpaper. "I still trust you," Mathilde said, and began to cry. "But I wish you had made all this a little easier."

HONG KONG

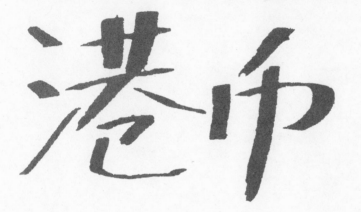

CHAPTER 20

MARK was glad, joyful in a balanced manner, maybe even happy. He had lunched well, with a drink before, wine on the side, and cognac afterward. He smoked a cigarette and stirred his coffee. The stewardess had cleared his tray, and the cup stood in the middle of its spotless baby-blue surface. The airplane's interior was gray-blue, the chairs were dark blue, and the sky was light blue. The different shades complemented each other perfectly. Everything is, Mark thought, the way it should be. All desires are fulfilled. The airplane left on time and will arrive on time. Meanwhile my own indicator touches zero, and the needle isn't even trembling. The perfection of an ideally created universe is mirrored in this undisturbed progress. The galaxies move faultlessly according to fixed laws. And not only do the mathematics of the supreme happening flow gently, their easy, endless sway is quite beautiful. Behold the empty sky in which everything is suspended; doesn't its pure azure emit continuous rays of splendor? Behold the Chinese sitting all around, with their identically cut and combed black hair, their spotless white shirts, their hats and caps exhibited along straight lines on shining racks. They're all leaning back in nice neat seats and returning to China to join another thousand million of the same, all diligently active, and cheerfully so, and forever so, to better their circumstances—be it communist or capitalist—and to increase the planet's wealth efficiently and enlarge the health and longevity of each individual, and nobody complains and everybody walks in step.

The airplane dropped into an air pocket, and Mark's coffee

cup fell over. The hats and the caps dropped out of the racks. A baby rolled through the aisle. Little Giant spilled some hot coffee on his fly and jumped up. He fell over against Syben, and Syben's elbow shot into Mathilde's arm. Mathilde woke up and looked around wide-eyed.

"Everything is under control," the pilot said bilingually. A stewardess brought small towels and a bottle of stain remover. The Chinese put their hats and caps back on the racks, and the baby was picked up and returned to its mother's arms.

Mark fell asleep. The concept of unlimited duplication stayed with him but had shifted its angle. He dreamed he was a sheep, trotting along cheerfully between other sheep. All sheep followed a ram. The ram was clearly recognizable because he was bigger than the sheep, and his curved horns had been dyed red. The sheep, guided by their leader, trotted toward a building. Mark could read; the other sheep couldn't. He read the inscription on the building: SLAUGH- TERHOUSE.

This is odd, Mark dreamed. Here we are, all of us, trotting along, neatly arranged in rows, six wide, infinitely long, all on our way to the slaughterhouse. Does nobody know that except me? The ram knew it, too, because he sharply changed direction just before he came to the building's yawning doors and trotted back, to find fresh populations of sheep. Mark veered away just in time, because he was close enough to see knives gleam, hatchets flash, blood spurt.

"Wake up," Little Giant said. "Your mouth is open and you're dribbling badly."

"Now everything is not under control," the pilot said bilingually. "You may have, after we hit the turbulence, felt a slight shock, because I lowered the landing gear. We are losing all hydraulic systems, and I would rather land on our wheels than our belly. We are about a thousand miles out of Hong Kong. By the time the engines no longer function, we will have reached our destination and have glided into the airport. The clouds that are now visible on each side of the airplane are formed by my release of our fuel, because I prefer empty tanks in case we crash. In view of the fire risk I'm asking you to extinguish your cigarettes. All drinks will be free from now on."

The Chinese mumbled, and the baby cried.

Alcohol flowed freely, but the stewardesses no longer smiled.

"What a pity," Little Giant said. "Just when things are going so well. But we did have rather a good time sorting stamps together."

Mathilde sat between the window and Syben. "You can hold my hand," Syben said. "I know that you would rather not spread your favors, but your position does not give you another option."

"You think this is the end?" Mark asked. "I had a funny dream just now. That could be a bad omen."

"Tell your dream," Little Giant said.

"So you managed to avoid the building?" Little Giant asked a little later.

"I did," Mark said. "The ram that tried to betray us made a left, and I a right. But all the other sheep went straight toward their deaths."

"But you didn't."

"I didn't."

"So it'll all come right in the end," Little Giant said, "because if you managed to save yourself, you will save us, too. We are a group and would have turned with you."

A stewardess offered a choice of liquor. Syben didn't react. He had equipped himself with earphones. The Modern Jazz Quartet played within his skull, working on a variation of Bach's Concerto for Two Harpsichords in C. Syben congratulated, while he listened, the heavenly employee responsible for directing fate at that precise moment. You excellent fellow, Syben thought, you have guessed correctly as to how I would prefer my exit. The music is excellent, every note is pure and in place and finds its resonance in my intimate observation. Perhaps I did waste too much time on doubt. My hypothesis that nothing at all can ever be of any intrinsic importance is not only clearly illustrated now but also confirmed in full. This is the third time that I'm being convinced of the relativity of everything, and the way in which the scene is set now must be ideal.

"Syben," Mathilde said.

Syben removed his earphones.

"I'm scared. Talk to me."

"What would you like me to talk about?"

"Oh my God," Mathilde said, "just look at that fog next to the plane. Is that really fuel?"

"We are flying," Syben said, "in the midst of a potential explosion."

"Oh my God. Please tell me a nice story. Your father would always tell me a comforting tale whenever I was not at ease with myself."

"A fairy tale?"

"Whatever you like, as long as it ends well."

"Once upon a time," Syben said, "there was a young man—or, rather, he was approaching thirty. He was a passenger on the bed of a truck, being driven through a bare plain in the former French colony of Chad. He was wearing a uniform and was armed with an American automatic rifle. *Wham!*"

"Oh my God," Mathilde said. "Did the fuel explode?"

"No, the truck hit a mine. It's cabin was torn apart, and the soldiers inside the cabin never had to do anything again, but the soldiers in the rear were still more or less okay. The young man was thrown into the air and dropped into the sand. He wasn't wounded, but he landed on his head and lost consciousness."

"Is this ending well?"

"Not yet. When he recovered, he was lying in a hut, and his ankles and wrists had been chained to a post that was hammered so deeply into the ground that he couldn't pull it out. A man wearing another type of uniform entered and gave him corn gruel and a bottle filled with water. That man, who was black, said that the young man—well, he was close to thirty—would be shot at dawn, together with the other mercenaries who had been thrown off the truck. That black man was the enemy, you see."

"And you were the young man?"

"Yes," Syben said, "and the enemy, an officer, liked jokes."

"And then, and then?"

Syben held up his earphones. "Wouldn't you rather listen to this? Good Bach."

"Does it have any drumming?"

Syben listened for a few seconds. "It has, careful and precise."

"I want to know how it went on with that young man."

"He was allowed," Syben said, "to contemplate, for the rest of the day and all of the night, what it would be like to feel a bullet enter his body, an aimed bullet, a one-two-*fire* bullet. That is not quite the same as a haphazard bullet."

"Oh my God," Mathilde said, "that fuel keeps on clouding up. Nasty smell, don't you think? And I can hardly hear the engines now. Do you think we'll make it? Surely a large, heavy airplane cannot glide. Won't it just fall? Would they be expecting us in Hong Kong? We should be able to land at once. Oh my God."

"Although a haphazard bullet can kill, too," Syben said. "But that wasn't bothering me too much then, that day and that night, because I was twisted around my post all of the time, dirtying my pants, and outside everything was going as usual. I could hear cars start up and drive away, goats bleating, and the sounds of female voices. Black female voices have beautiful side sounds, like a saxophone that is being played well. You hear the melody, but underneath, or in between, other sounds fit in and around what they're saying to you. I thought then that music exists thanks to the silence, and is no more than lines around the silence, and that life outlines death."

"But the end is good," Mathilde said, "because you're sitting next to me."

"Yes, but I didn't know that things would go on. In the morning the enemy showed up again, and I was taken outside and tied to a fence, opposite a row of soldiers, neat warriors in clean shorts and Sam Browne belts across their tunics, and the sun came up and I looked into the barrels of their rifles, and each rifle had a chromium-plated bolt that shone in the early light. The officer counted up to two."

"Why didn't they shoot?"

"Because they were jokers. I was untied again and taken away."

"And you escaped?"

"A little later," Syben said.

"Did you have to kill a lot of people?"

"I don't quite know how many, but there must have been a few; that was part of the exercise. Have another drink."

"One more tale?"

"You choose the subject."

"About a nice little animal."

"An abalone is a nice little animal," Syben said. "The skipper paid me a quarter each, and there were hundreds of them on the same rock sometimes."

"What is an abalone?"

"A mollusk that lives in a mother-of-pearl shell, off the Cape Coast in South Africa. Catching them was quite easy, they told me, but it took a little time to get used to conditions. I had to wear a rubber suit and goggles, and they put the snout of a tube into my mouth. I got pushed overboard and sank until I stood on the bottom. The abalone live down there. You pry them loose with a screwdriver that is strapped to your wrist and drop them in a net. The more you catch the more you earn, but the divers fight each other for the right rocks and will puncture your suit with their screwdrivers or squeeze your air tube."

"What terrible men they must be."

"People are no good," Syben said, "and sharks are no good at all."

"They were there, too?"

"Oh yes, usually the most evil variety, big whites, and they're always around to see what you're doing."

"And they attack?"

"They squeeze themselves past you as if they want to be petted, but their skin is like sandpaper and they try to rip you open. They will attack as soon as they smell blood."

"We're going down," Mathilde said. "I hope that pilot won't get nervous. The engines are out now. He'll have to land the plane quietly, and then we'll roll down the runway easily enough."

"One of the divers was bleeding, and a shark came for him. When they turn on their backs, then you know they're serious, because they can bite better when they turn upside down. We had given the alarm by jerking our ropes and were being pulled up. Sharks have a lot of big teeth."

"But nothing happened, right?"

"One of the divers lost his leg."

"But it wasn't your leg, right?"

"I took an eye out of a shark, with my screwdriver. That wasn't nice, but he kept bumping me; that wasn't nice either. Isn't this great?"

The airplane flew low over the sea, alongside a junk under three patched sails. The ship's size about equaled that of the plane. A wizened old man waved from the junk's high rear deck.

"Charming old man of the sea," Mathilde said. "He doesn't know we are about to crash."

Off-white buildings towered behind the junk. The tallest reflected the sky from rows of round windows. Behind the building were others, hundreds of square columns, mathematical cubes projected against dark chaotic and fertile green, growing on primordial rock, forming mountains with their tops sliced off.

"Welcome in Hong Kong," the pilot said. "They're waiting for us. There's foam on the runway to soften our landing, and there will be elastic cables to catch this machine." The pilot's voice trembled. "We'll be just fine."

"Just land the thing," Little Giant said.

"Hold on," the pilot murmured.

"Look," Mathilde said. "Ambulances, fire trucks, flashing lights—oh my God."

The plane landed easily enough, sliding on thick foam, caught neatly by cables.

The passengers watched while the pilot, staring straight

ahead, walked down the staircase, found some clean runway, knelt, prayed.

"He thanks his god," Mark said.

"Good," Syben said, "I thank his god, too. I thank him for kidding."

"This is a solemn moment," Little Giant said, "and perhaps I may use it by asking you a question."

Mark dried his face, Mathilde bit her handkerchief, and Syben looked at a cigarette that he couldn't light because the plane was still soaked with wasted fuel. The stewardess addressed the passengers through a bullhorn. "Don't smoke, please. Enter the building as soon as possible."

"I would like to know," Little Giant said, "which one of you is the thief."

Nobody answered.

"Now what were we supposed to do here?" Mark asked after they had passed customs and immigration.

"Hotel?" a Chinese asked.

"How are you doing, Mathilde?" Syben asked in the taxi. Mathilde smiled. "Very well, thank you, darling."

"We aren't going to be intimate, now are we?" Little Giant asked.

"You're a darling, too, and Mark is included. Do you remember that business about the matriarchy?"

"The what?" Mark asked.

"One of you mentioned that in Tunisia. There are societies in which the woman heads the family, and she can have more than one husband. Some of them have as many as three."

"Mathilde is making us a proposal," Little Giant said. "Now look at those alleys and all those crazy signs that nobody can read and the cops wearing shorts. This can't be right; maybe we should go back to the airport."

"Yes. I am making a proposal. We rent a simple little house, where the country is beautiful and money still has value, and I will do the housekeeping and you will go for walks, and maybe read the paper. If we are careful, we can keep doing that forever, peacefully, and in harmony."

"And can we all go to bed with you?"

"Yes, Mark. But not all the time, of course, I will have to rest every now and then, and all of you will have to help me washing up."

"Not a bad idea," Syben said.

"We're here to sell stamps," Little Giant said, "and every distraction will make us waste time. That's silly talk, Mathilde. Cut it out."

"Here hotel," the driver said.

"To work," Little Giant said.

CHAPTER 21

"WHAT are you doing there?" Little Giant asked.

"I'm looking at the boats," Syben said, "but they seem rather to be houses. I don't think they ever go anywhere."

"Sampans," Little Giant said.

Syben shook his head at a smiling and nodding young woman who walked toward their bench. "But that lady is only trying to be polite," Little Giant said.

"A prostitute," Syben said. "She must be about the tenth I've seen, and I've only been here a few minutes. Perhaps I wouldn't mind, but I don't understand where they would take me to. Those sampans house families. How can those ladies take care of their customers when everybody is watching?"

Little Giant sighed. "There might be curtains. Do you know that the city continues on the other side of the water?"

"We are in Kowloon; the other shore is called Victoria. You'll have to take the ferry," Syben said. "I checked the south side out yesterday. It's very clever to split a city by water. One has a chance to lose it all while on the water, before getting busy again." Syben got up. "Come along, there's another lot aiming for us. With all these black-haired people around we stand out too much. They think that we are lecherous tourists."

Little Giant trotted next to his brother. "We don't stand out when we're walking? I've been to Victoria, too. There seems to be more going on over there than here. Narrow alleys and hellish traffic, but not uninteresting. Quite a lot to see."

"But did you see an auction?"

"I did," Little Giant said, "I even went inside. They're selling twice a week, and I was allowed to view the offered stock, if I kept my hands behind my back. Nice collections, but nothing at all compared to what we will be showing them."

"Good afternoon," Syben said.

The woman was middle-aged and smiled at him from a friendly, wrinkled face. She waved a soup ladle, spoke Chinese, pointed at the waterside, and moved her hands as if she were stuffing rice into her mouth with chopsticks.

"Shall we follow her?" Little Giant asked. "I wouldn't mind eating something, and she has a good smell."

The restaurant boat was squeezed between other sampans. The woman ladled noodle soup into bowls and served deep-fried fish croquettes. There were no other customers. A white puppy wagged its tail at the guests, and a canary sang from a bamboo cage. In the neighboring boats daily life carried on. Transistor radios mingled their brassy music as peddlers rowed alongside in dinghies. Colorful laundry dried on lines, women scrubbed decks or mended clothes, a child lithely jumping from boat to boat came home carrying groceries, and another child paddled away in a plastic bathtub.

"No unnecessary wealth," Syben said. "Apparently nobody's hungry, and they aren't dressed in rags. How simple life can be. Don't you think that we complicate matters too much?"

"I'm selling stamps," Little Giant said, "and that auction gave me hives on my back. Nothing but Chinese spoken all around, and they can rip you off while they're looking into your eyes. I don't even dare to leave my goods, maybe they'll give me a used cinema ticket instead of a receipt. What *did* I get myself into?"

The woman broiled a small flounder on charcoal. "Now look at that," Syben said. "Simplicity in its purest form. That lady throws a line overboard and catches a fish. She rips out its innards and subsequently prepares a tasty meal.

She scoops a few dollars from the water and can concern herself with her spiritual welfare for the rest of the week."

"Excellent flounder," Little Giant said, "in a gourmet sauce. Yes, if you please ma'am, a bowl of rice will complete the meal very nicely."

Little Giant was given tea as well.

"You think they have a toilet here?"

"No," Syben said. "It'll have to go overboard, and that's overdoing it again. Too much simplicity, perhaps, but this should make one think. We rush about like gold-assed flies, juggling unpronounceable amounts of money, and here this dear old thing prepares a sustaining meal for just a few pennies."

He paid, and balancing on boards and swaying decks, they maneuvered themselves back to the shore.

"Where is a toilet?"

"Over there?"

Little Giant looked at little buildings indicated by Syben's arm. Each store had its own sign. Some even dangled several. "I can't make sense out of those copulating worms," Little Giant said. "It's hard to believe that they're really letters."

"So, look through the windows; one of those buildings will be a café. I'll wait here for you. I've got to think for a while."

Syben found a protected spot between a bright red mailbox and a streetlight on a slender post and submerged himself in ponderings while a steady stream of pedestrians flowed behind him and another mass of cyclists and puttering cars, moving at about the same speed, pushed itself ahead past the sidewalk.

It took a little while before Little Giant, struggling between men in narrow trousers and white open-necked shirts, and young women wearing skirts slit open on both sides, found him again.

"I really thought that most people were white," Little Giant said, "but that is probably not true at all. How many Chinese are there, do you think?"

"A billion."

"And the earth's population?"

"Four, I believe."

"Perhaps everything I have figured out isn't true."

"I have thought that often," Syben said. "That's because we learn wrong from the beginning, and after that it's easier to keep carrying all that faulty information."

"But I did find a store dealing in stamps. Care to come for a look? Perhaps we'll learn something about prices."

Little Giant pushed Syben to a small store. Syben greeted an older gentleman who was leaving the hovel.

"Good day, Mr. Sobryne," the man said.

Little Giant's mouth opened wide. He closed it again. "Do you speak Dutch?"

"I certainly do." The man appeared to be in his seventies and wore an old-fashioned shantung suit, complete with waistcoat, watch chain, straw hat, and silver-knobbed cane. "I originate in Curaçao." He bowed down to Little Giant and extended his hand. "Da Costa is the name."

"Sobryne."

"I see. You two are related."

"We are brothers," Syben said, and patted Little Giant's shoulder. "Mr. Da Costa is staying in our hotel, and he and I had breakfast together this morning."

"You are a stamp collector?" Little Giant asked.

"Well," Da Costa said, "in a way, perhaps, if I have nothing else to do. Can I offer the gentlemen a cup of coffee?"

The world is too big for me, Little Giant thought while he followed Syben and Da Costa. Curaçao, is it? An island, but I have no idea how far away, and here I am on another island. There are a thousand times a thousand times a thousand Chinese all around me, and this Mr. Da Costa, whose name is Portugese and who speaks Dutch, must have had a black mother. Shall I go crazy right now, or can I still wait a bit? What is he doing here?

"What are you doing here?"

Da Costa's heavy eyelids lifted a little. "That is a long story, Mr. Sobryne."

"I would like to hear it very much."

"Then I will abbreviate its contents. I earn my living by manufacturing and selling textiles. I once did that on my own island, but the cost of manufacturing became too high, so I moved here. When the cost of manufacturing became too high here also, I moved to Taiwan. In Taiwan, ach, it is a monotonous story . . . you really want to hear it?"

"Yes, yes," Little Giant said.

"In Taiwan the cost of manufacturing is rising, too. It is a cruel world, Mr. Sobryne. Costs increase because wages go up, but those who earn the high wages do not want to buy the products they make themselves because they're too expensive. But now the Chinese mainland is opening up duty-free manufacturing zones, and I have applied for permission to build a factory in Shenzen. If my application is granted, I will be able to compete again."

"Schenzen," Little Giant said. "Is that far from here?"

"No, but I fly out there once a week to inquire if my form might have been stamped already."

"And meanwhile you're living here?"

"Yes, but my house is in Taiwan, but Taiwan is too far out, again."

"My brother lives on a dike," Syben said, "and weaves baskets, but now he's selling stamps."

The old gentleman took his time to sort out this information. He pushed his wide-brimmed hat back on his head, placed his elbows carefully on the table, intertwined his fingers, and rested his chin on his knuckles. His large, widely slanting eyes gleamed, and his nostrils extended a little. He directed himself to Little Giant, no longer in a conversational tone of voice but somewhat hoarsely. He smiled, showing healthy pink gums holding strong, perfect teeth, so that the indignation contained in his sharp question might be compensated by kindness. "You have come from Holland to Hong Kong to sell *postage stamps*?"

"I have a lot of them, Mr. Da Costa," Little Giant said.

Syben was smiling, too. "And of excellent quality."

"You have to tell me more about your proposition."

Little Giant explained while Syben, listening, studied Da

Costa. It is strange, Syben thought, but I recognize myself in this man, although all we have in common seems to be the length of our bodies. He has Einstein's nose, Spinoza's eyes, and the Modern Jazz Quartet's color. He is from another culture, or from a number of other cultures, but even so, there is no essential difference between the two of us. He has developed himself more than I, but he must have made a choice once that I made, too, and that opened up a direction that will take me to his point. This exceptional being will not allow himself to be touched by overall accepted rules. He's indifferent, even though he plays the everyday game that he refuses to be part of. He's here, but he's not here at the same time.

Da Costa made Little Giant finish his tale, helping him along by straightening things out when Little Giant became confused.

"You do know about stamps," Little Giant said.

"A little," Da Costa said, "but I haven't acquainted myself with the material as merchandise, although I do own a few albums of countries where I happened to live. Each country shows itself, or perhaps betrays itself, in her stamps, and not only in the portrayed pictures or in the frames that decorate their edges but even in their denominating figures. I like to sit quietly at times and study the information that my collection conveys. Stamps are like windows in a secretive house, and one sometimes can look in quite clearly."

"You also collect Chinese stamps?"

"I do," Da Costa said. "Some more coffee, my friend?"

"Yes, please. Perhaps you can advise me on how to sell off my goods?"

Da Costa smiled. "I beg your pardon; I had forgotten again that you're only interested in profit. An old man likes to philosophize, but the deeper ruminations do not make the cash register ring. You are planning to stay here for a long time?"

"We cannot stay too long," Syben said.

Da Costa thanked the waitress in Chinese and pushed the coffee cups away. "Then you will have to make use of the auctions. I have a number of reliable contacts in Hong Kong and may be able to be of service, with pleasure, I might add. The authorities of the mainland are too slow for me, and all this hanging around here is boring me a little."

Little Giant looked through the window. He read some of the English signs in between the maze of Chinese characters depicted in various styles: KAISER RESTAURANT, TUNG SHUN HING STORE, SHANGHAI NEW SAM YOUNG STORE, KENTUCKY FRIED CHICKEN, MAN HING & CO, COCA-COLA, XIM, WO HOP. "Wo Hop," Little Giant said aloud. He groaned in his weakness. "Ach, Mr. Da Costa."

"Yes, Mr. Sobryne?"

Little Giant raised his shoulders. "It's all so weird here. All those signs and those strange people, and living on boats and all."

"Not all of them, Mr. Sobryne. Some Chinese live in palaces, although most of them are restrained in small quarters. I ran into a man who lives in a cupboard the other day, and a clerk who served me yesterday said he exists in a packing crate on a roof, but that may be more comfortable than the sampans they have exiled the others to."

"The others? But aren't they all Chinese?"

"No, no, Mr. Sobryne. Here, too, several peoples mingle. There are also the Hakka, the Hoklo and the Tanka, second class citizens, remnants of earlier civilizations. Once quite important, especially the Hakka, who were so active and diligent that they caused the troubles of 1865 and were nearly exterminated. Twenty million dead, Mr. Sobryne."

Da Costa offered scented cigarettes from a worn gold case. "This is the country of unimaginable figures. All of southern China was on fire. And now the Hakka live on little boats and float on their own garbage, or in shanty towns in the jungle of northern Borneo. Postage stamps, you were saying."

"Quite something you have here," Da Costa said an hour later, bowed over Little Giant's albums.

"But how do I get rid of all this?" Little Giant asked.

Da Costa scratched his back. "Can I sit down a moment?"

Mark fetched a chair. "Would you like a drink?" Mathilde asked.

"A planter's rum, please."

Da Costa's long, muscular fingers spread on his thighs. The segments seemed to move independently. He's really stroking Mathilde, Syben thought, because he has seen how lovely she is. At his age desires are fulfilled in a more abstract way. But I have that, too, even now, at *my* age. Syben looked out of the window. A Rolls Royce was parked outside the hotel. Syben saw the long, stately line of the impeccably polished car and the agile figure of its uniformed driver, who was opening the door for a fat, cigar-smoking man. I don't need a Rolls Royce, Syben thought, but it should be a pity if nobody needed one, because then I would never see such a splendid vehicle.

"If you really would like to assist us with this business," Mark said, "we would gladly pay a commission."

Da Costa leafed through an album. "A commission? Well, perhaps we can discuss that later." He pointed at a stamp. "This one we should study under ultraviolet light. If it doesn't contain a watermark, it should be worth six hundred dollars. And there was something about the perforation, I believe. I own a cheap copy, worth about ten cents."

"Do you have a lamp with ultraviolet light?" Little Giant asked.

"I can borrow one and probably get hold of a perforation measure, too. Let me see now, what shall I do? I can recommend a trustworthy auctioneer in Victoria, and we can visit my acquaintance together to see how the business is done, but if you opt for that possibility, you hardly need me."

"You think we will realize a sizable amount?"

"Oh, surely, but the game can be played in a more intelligent way."

"We would like to pay a commission," Mark said. "You know the local customs and can protect us against our own ignorance."

Da Costa drank his rum. "You know, the taxes here are not unreasonable, and the authorities do not meddle much, but even so, the local nabobs do not like to advertise their wealth. Whatever is auctioned in Kowloon and Victoria comes to everybody's notice."

"Illegal money?"

"Black money, as we call it here, Mr. Sobryne, but money should be transparent. Real wealth has no color."

˙ Mark smiled knowingly.

"You can look through money; its substance is quite immaterial. And the wealthy would like to keep it that way because they want to stay rich for as long as possible. In Macao . . ."

Little Giant plucked at his collar. "Now where is Macao?"

"Not here, Mr. Sobryne. Macao is on the mainland, Portugese territory, well out of the way of most laws, a resort where life can be very pleasurable, a heavenly sphere reached by hovercraft—across the sea without ever touching the waves."

"There are auctions there, too?"

"Yes, Mr. Sobryne, and whatever takes place there is invisible here." Da Costa rubbed his high forehead. "I will have to go and see if my connections are still active; everything is subject to change, is it not? I haven't been to Macao for a good many years." He got up. "Allow me a few days."

"Ten percent," Mark said, and opened the door for his guest. "Nothing is free, Mr. Da Costa. We would not like you to incur expenses you cannot cover."

Da Costa stood near the door and bowed to Mathilde. The gold of his watch chain and in his teeth shone. His hoarse voice filled the ample room. "I do have to do something with my time, and stamps interest me. Just let me be for a little while, and then we'll see if we can come to business."

"A gentleman," Mathilde said after Mark had closed the door. "More adventurous than your father but of the same class, I would say." She looked at Mark's shoes. "And he wears polished shoes. Gentlemen always look neat."

Little Giant ran about in the room. "What to do? What to do? Shouldn't we hide the albums in the hotel safe? Maybe they're worth more than two hundred thousand dollars in Macao. Who has a map?"

Syben unfolded the map. "Here, a little to the left from where we are." He placed his finger on the measurements below the map and moved his hand up. "Fifty kilometers from Hong Kong? Won't be much more than that. Hovercraft are fast. Should take an hour or so."

"I can see those bales of hash floating in the Mediterranean again," Little Giant said. "This is going to go the same way. That boat will sink, and all the stamps will get away, with their white sides up, forming a thin line right to the horizon, very visible in the moonlight."

"A good image, but rather psychotic," Mark said. "What's wrong, Mathilde?"

Mathilde lay on the couch.

"Aren't you feeling well?" Syben asked. "You look pale. Would you like to go to your room?"

"I feel dizzy."

"So do I," Little Giant said. "That's because of that stupid airplane, and also because of all of the hectic goings-on here. I've never seen such crowded streets and at all times of the day. Rotterdam is a village compared to this. I thought Holland was full and that our overpopulation was to blame for our bad manners. It's a miracle that people here still manage to be polite. When you put too many mice in a cage, they eat each other."

"I feel sick, too," Mathilde said.

"I'll take you to your room," Mark said. "You need a rest."

"Would you mind staying with me for a while?" Mathilde asked in the corridor. "I really feel unwell; everything is turning about me. I wish Little Giant hadn't said that about the mice."

"Stop running to and fro," Syben said to Little Giant. "This will turn out all right. Da Costa arrived just in time, and now we can take a few days off. If he's kind enough to take our work away from us, we can observe the city and its environment. One doesn't go to China every day."

CHAPTER 22

"AGAIN?" Mark asked.

"Please," Mathilde said softly. "The bucket, Mark." He lifted her head and cleaned her mouth with a wet facecloth.

"Feeling better? Now be a good girl and lie down."

"I'm not a good girl," Mathilde whispered. "I'm all dirty. I wish you didn't have to see me like this, but I feel so ill."

Mark carried the bucket to the bathroom. "It doesn't matter at all. I'm sick too at times, and you vomit in a most refined manner."

Mathilde tried to smile. Mark washed the bucket out in the bath. Right. Everything is in order again. Would you like to change your nightgown?"

"Yes, but I don't find it easy to move."

"Up with your arms," Mark said. "Away with that rag. Now put this one on, a very nice garment, with stripes. It'll make you look slender."

"Am I that fat?" Mathilde whispered.

"No, you are a perfect beauty, but I am fat, and that's why I always wear shirts with vertical stripes, so that my belly won't show too much."

"You're in excellent shape," Mathilde said. "All you have is a bit of a tum. If you exercise a little, it'll be gone in a few weeks."

"I don't like exercise."

"Play ball?"

"Basketball?" Mark asked. "I used to be good at that, but I got too busy. When I get back to Rotterdam, I'll play ball again."

172

"Yes," Mathilde whispered. "I used to like to play hand-ball, but I can't imagine now that I ever ran on a field. I think I'll never be out of bed again."

Mark ordered tea over the telephone. "It'll be here in a minute, and then you can take another pill. The doctor thinks that you're suffering from food poisoning."

"I'm not."

"Why not? There's just about everything in Chinese food. Eggs that have been rotting underground for a hundred years, whale snot, monkey's ears . . ."

"The bucket," whispered Mathilde.

"I am sorry," Mark said, after he had wiped Mathilde's mouth again. "I am a worthless nurse. Would you like to sleep a little now?"

"If you stay with me."

Mark read the paper. Mathilde mumbled in her sleep. He bowed down over her. "Da Costa," Mathilde whispered.

She woke up again an hour later.

"You said 'Da Costa' in your sleep."

Mathilde turned toward him. "Yes, that's quite possible. I was dreaming about that man. He wanted to harm me. Some sort of smoky fog was coming out of his body and I couldn't see anymore, and he picked me up and carried me away."

"Da Costa seemed a dignified old gentleman to me, and very helpful, too."

"Where is he now?" Mathilde asked.

Mark looked at his watch. "He'll be in Macao, with Little Giant and Syben. I saw him in the corridor last night. He said that Macao has a number of auctions and that stamps are sold there once every week."

Mathilde tried to show interest. "Did he have time to study our collections?"

"Certainly. Little Giant was so excited that he was summersaulting all through the suite. It seems we have more valuable stamps than we thought. All sorts of overprints on air postage, and a pagoda upside down, and even a *tête-bêche*."

"What is that?"

"Head to tail."

"I don't understand."

"Two identical stamps attached head to tail; how that can be I don't know, either. A Sun Yat-sen up and a Sun Yat-sen down, with the perforation in between."

"And that's worth a lot of money?"

"Most rarities are pricey."

"Are you going to stay here tonight, Mark?"

He stroked her cheek softly. "Nothing will give me greater pleasure."

"Good," Mathilde said. "I keep having nightmares, and when I wake up and see you, I feel quiet again."

"But what are you dreaming about all the time?"

"Always about Da Costa."

"You're probably in love," Mark said, "because you are attracted to old men. And Da Costa is an imposing fellow, I realized that again yesterday when I saw him striding in the corridor. No, 'striding' isn't the right word, either. Instead of shuffling, like most old men do, Da Costa seems to glide. And his voice is remarkable, too. Every time he says something, my spine tingles."

"I feel it in my stomach," Mathilde said, "and lower still. When I met Da Costa, he fascinated me, but now I feel frightened whenever I think of him."

"Time for the next pill."

"I'd rather have tea with a little dry rice."

"Excellent," Mark said. "You are getting better."

Mathilde dozed off. Mark held on to her hand. She opened her eyes again. "You're really very sweet to me. If I wasn't so sick, I wouldn't mind kissing you. I have to go to the bathroom again."

She got up and leaned on Mark's arm. He walked her to the washstand and watched her clean her teeth and comb her hair.

She smiled. "Now."

"What do you mean?"

"Kiss." She embraced him, and he held her softly.

"Would you like more?" Mathilde asked.

"I would like it all, but not now. You are still too weak; the doctor recommends absolute rest."

"Yes," Mathilde said, and stumbled back to her bed. She dropped down and Mark arranged the covers.

"You're really kind, aren't you?" Mathilde asked.

"If I am," Mark said, "it must be due to recent developments. I have always been a puffed-up toad. I'm beginning to see that now. Our adventures may be costly, but they are not quite useless. When I observe Little Giant and Syben, I admit that they're further along than I, but even a puffed-up toad can make spiritual progress."

Mathilde caressed Mark's hair.

"You *are* nice," Mathilde said. "You remind me of somebody."

"Of my father?"

"Yes," Mathilde said, "but I didn't want to say that. It's silly to compare people, because everyone is different and does not have the same opportunities to project what he is."

Mark walked to the bathroom and took a shower. When he came back it was almost dark in the room. Mathilde was asleep. He lay down next to her. Mathilde's hand rested in his and pushed softly against his forehead. Mark slept deeply and didn't move, but Mathilde's body trembled and shook. She was mumbling again.

CHAPTER 23

LITTLE Giant and Syben, each holding a suitcase, stood next to Da Costa. Spray streaking against the hovercraft's windscreen blotted out most of the view.

"There is the Pearl River," Da Costa said. "In the old days, when even the largest ships could enter the port, it was important, but now it's all silted up so that only small fishing craft and the Hong Kong ferry can get in."

"This boat will make it, eh?" Little Giant asked.

"It's standing on its aprons," Syben said. "I never saw anything like this before, quite an invention. Look, palm trees."

"The gangway is down," Da Costa said. "Let's get off. Macao is more tropical than Hong Kong. This here is an earthly heaven of parks and old Portugese architecture."

"A pink house," Little Giant said, "and those over there are yellow. How merry, between all the greenery."

"How would you like to go to the auction? We can take a taxi, catch a bus, or hire three-wheeled rickshaws, but they only seat two."

The rickshaws, moving soundlessly through the lush cityscape, were cycled along by muscular Chinese under straw hats. Da Costa sat next to Little Giant.

"A true paradise," Little Giant said. "I've got nothing against Rotterdam, and I don't like to complain, but all that gray rain and those long, narrow streets with clouds on top sometimes get too much for me. This is the way people should live, in the sun, with flowering vines on the walls and fruit trees in the gardens and hammocks and rocking chairs on the veranda."

"A paradise earned with smuggled gold and gambling, Mr. Sobryne. You're still on earth."

"I'd rather forget that for a moment."

"And over there," Da Costa said, "is Red China, land of slaving ants in blue overalls, and brotherly love, but if you don't do exactly as Big Brother says, you will be in big trouble."

"It's all right here," Little Giant said, "and I'm here." He rubbed his hands together. "Life is great. Hurrah."

The rickshaw parked in front of a low pavilion with a roof supported by golden dragons. A freshly painted sign hung from red cords in the gate: WONG'S AUCTION, STAMPS AND COINS.

"Today it's only stamps," Da Costa said to Syben, "and my old friend Wong assures me that all important dealers and collectors from Hong Kong and Taiwan will be bidding. We have agreed that your stock will be sold once the buyers' interest has been properly provoked."

"I do appreciate your help," Syben said. "We would never have found this place by ourselves."

Da Costa wanted to pick up a suitcase, but Little Giant was too fast for him.

"I can still carry weights," Da Costa said. "I play a little golf. And you don't have to be grateful at all. Without me you would have sold your merchandise in Victoria, and they do realize attractive prices out there, but here you'll get some fifteen to twenty percent more; the clients are more courageous in Macao."

An old gentleman in a silken robe bowed his welcome. Da Costa pointed at Little Giant and Syben and spoke in rapid Chinese. He directed himself to the brothers. "Mr. Wong speaks little English but understands the language fairly well."

Wong received his clients in a back room and looked at Little Giant's albums while two girls brought in tea.

"Mr. Wong is very contented," Da Costa said. "He says that your merchandise is A-1 fancy."

Behind them the murmuring of many voices became audible. "A lot of people about," Little Giant said happily.

"Many clients," Syben said in English.

Wong tugged at his white goatee. "Much good business today. Much happy you came."

"What a jolly old chap," Little Giant said. "Isn't it nice to deal with happy people?"

"Who knows what they're doing," Da Costa said.

The auction began. A dozen Chinese buyers were bidding on albums and stock books held up by an assistant while Wong advertised their contents in an impressive chanting voice. The digging was slow and the amounts modest.

"Nothing much there, so far," Da Costa whispered, "but he'll mix in a few good items soon to get some tension. Ah, look, there's something now."

The assistant showed a single stamp, carefully held by his tweezers.

"A ten-dollar from 1915, unused, very fine," whispered Da Costa. "A thousand dollars in the stock catalog." He waved at Wong. "Seven hundred dollars."

"Do you want to buy it?" Little Giant asked.

"At seven hundred dollars it would be a gift, but it'll go for more. I want to help Wong a little; if the bidding starts high, the price will shoot up quickly."

"Eight hundred," a Chinese in a Mao suit shouted.

"Hong Kong dollars?" Little Giant asked.

Da Costa shook his head. "No, American. The American dollar is still the world's currency, and here the buying is international."

"Eleven hundred," a Chinese in shirtsleeves and suspenders said quietly.

"But that's more than the catalog price," Syben said.

Da Costa nodded. "The stamp is truly rare, and the catalog only gives an indication."

"Twelve hundred? Do I hear anyone else?"

Wong's gavel hit the table. The gentleman in the Mao suit was the buyer.

"Now we'll have some run-of-the-mill stuff again," Da Costa said, "and then he'll be starting on yours. Wong prefers to sell album by album, and there'll be a short break so that the buyers can have a last look. You wouldn't mind that, would you now?"

"As long as I get tea," Little Giant said, "because my tongue is sticking to the roof of my mouth. My nerves have sucked up all my spittle."

The first and least interesting album was shown and changed hands for twenty thousand dollars. The second album realized a little more, and the third, in which Mark had inserted some variations and misprints, went for forty.

"We are over a hundred thousand," Syben said, "and the unused stamps haven't even been touched yet."

Little Giant sat down and read the slip of paper that Wong's assistant passed along. "Two hundred sixty-three thousand dollars?"

"That's what it says," Syben said.

"Indeed," Da Costa said, "but you will get a little less because Wong's rice bowl needs filling, too."

"And ten percent for you," Syben said. "You certainly earned your commission. What an amazing lot of money. *Postage stamps.*" Syben shook his head.

The auction continued while Da Costa accompanied the brothers to the back room. The girls brought tea and crackers. "We can wait here for a while so that Wong can write out the check. You might be better off cashing the check here and buying another one in Kowloon later on, at the Chase Manhattan office. Or, if you prefer, we can arrange to have the money transferred to your bank in Holland."

"Absolutely incredible," Little Giant said, "more than a quarter of a million dollars. This is true treasure."

Syben had trouble keeping his eyes open. His cane chair was unexpectedly comfortable.

"I'm sleepy," Little Giant said.

"That's because of the sea wind and the tension. Why don't you close your eyes for a while, I'll wake you up when Wong comes in."

Syben felt himself floating away on Da Costa's low, powerful voice. The voice became a gigantic black wave pushing him to bright orange fire, flaming on the horizon. The last image that Syben saw, before he woke up hours later, was the grinning faces of the Indian guru and the mercenary sergeant in Chad. "You always have to pay attention," the guru and the sergeant said, sharing their voices.

"Where are we?" Little Giant asked, groping about in the empty room. "Wong? Da Costa?"

"They went home for dinner," Syben said, "and the auction wasn't for real."

"What, what?" Little Giant asked.

"A theater performance," Syben said, "and we have lost our merchandise." He felt his jacket and pulled out his wallet. "You still have yours?"

"Here," Little Giant said.

"Any money in it?"

"Yes."

"I still have the hovercraft tickets," Syben said, "so we can make it back to Hong Kong. No suitcases to carry this time."

"God . . ."

"Don't curse," Syben said. "You're the third in a row. Mathilde happened to be unlucky, and Mark overdid things a bit, and you ran across a bad man, purely evil. Come to think of it, that's quite an experience."

On the way back Little Giant sat next to a Catholic priest, an older man in a threadbare monk's habit tied with a wide leather belt.

"You don't look too happy," the priest said.

"I don't understand you."

The priest was Portugese, but he also spoke English.

"I'm unhappy," Little Giant said, "because I've just lost a lot of money."

"Been gambling, have you?"

"No, it was taken from me."

"Did you visit the police?"

Little Giant shrugged his shoulders. "In Macao?"

"We do employ police in the colonies," the priest said, "and I have been told that they manage to maintain order."

"My thief will be out of your colony by now," Little Giant said.

"Are you poor now?"

"I still have a few pennies."

"Moments of calamity are very suitable for prayer," the priest said kindly.

Little Giant looked at the priest angrily. "I don't believe in your god, and your Christian saints can take a walk. They've never done a thing for me."

The hovercraft moored. The priest and Little Giant walked together to the customs gate. "Over there," the priest said.

Little Giant looked.

"She's a saint, too," the priest said.

Little Giant stopped in front of the shrine the priest indicated and stared at the image of a young woman shielded by a golden roof. Her large, calm eyes beneath an elaborate hairdo focused on faraway glory, while her full-tilted lips smiled mysteriously. "*Tyen Hou*," the venerable monk said, "the goddess of the sky, assigned to lessen the suffering of this planet."

"She'll only take care of Chinese," Little Giant said.

"I wouldn't say that. Her compassion is not limited to this country, and the goddess possesses supreme concentration and unlimited powers. When you direct your prayer to her, she will certainly listen."

A small dog brushed past Little Giant's leg. "I might as well talk to the dog. He'll be listening too, eh, Fido?"

The mongrel looked up, wagging its broken tail.

"The dog cannot help you much, because he has been programmed fairly simply, but the goddess is not bound by limitations. She can help you and will certainly do so if you open yourself to her. I wish you a good day." The priest walked on.

"Hello?" Syben asked.

"I'll be busy for a moment," Little Giant said. "Let me be. I'll join you shortly."

Little Giant prayed.

Syben waited.

"You weren't praying, were you?" Syben asked.

"Nothing to do with you what I was doing," Little Giant said. "And now we will be returning to the hotel. I'll sell the mess that Da Costa said wasn't worth the trouble at a real auction in Victoria, and then we'll get the hell out of here."

"Don't get upset," Syben said. "You were clever enough to keep some of your capital on the side, in case of unforseen trouble, and my share of the inheritance is still safely in Rotterdam."

"I'm not upset," Little Giant said, and kicked a pebble. The pebble was cemented to the sidewalk's surface.

CHAPTER 24

"IF I see one more stamp," Little Giant said, "I will vomit."
Mathilde placed a full sheet on the table. "Don't throw up
on this. Mark and I found it in between the remnants. I
didn't even know it was there. I probably bought it from one
of those funny little boys. Aren't they lovely?"

"No," Little Giant said.

"The seventy-three-shent overprint on the orange airplane
from 1932?"

"Cent," Little Giant said. "Only in America they put a
stroke through the *c*."

Mark pointed. "Look again, Little Giant. While you two
were in Macao, we checked it in the catalog. No watermark
and a perforation of fourteen over two centimeters. These
stamps are worth six hundred dollars each."

"Get away with your rubbish," Little Giant said.

"And there are fifty to a sheet. Thirty thousand dollars,
Little Giant."

"Bah," Little Giant said. "But how could it be? It was just
like I told you, Mark. You can ask Syben. A lovely pavilion,
with a sign, and completely furnished, buyers all over the
joint, an auctioneer waving a gavel. And suddenly it was all
gone."

"There was a girl, too, giving you some tea. Don't you
have a headache?"

"No. And we woke up on the bare floor. Where is Da
Costa?"

"I just asked in the lobby. He checked out this morning
without leaving a forwarding address."

"And taking everything I had."

"Don't exaggerate," Mark said. "You still have your cottage on the dike and the twenty thousand dollars you kept apart, and now another thirty thousand once we sell that sheet of rare overprints."

"Please," Little Giant said, "don't talk nonsense Mark."

Mark was proved right. The sheet was sold for close to thirty thousand. The remnants realized a few hundred. There was still some money.

"But where is Syben?" Little Giant asked. "I haven't seen him since we returned."

Syben walked along the shore. Revenge, Syben thought, has nothing to do with indifference, and detachment is the greatest good. I don't care about getting even, and I'm walking here between dirty water on one side and ruined hovels on the other because I'm studying life in all of its manifestations, as an observer who has freed himself of whatever holds others in its grasp. I'm not looking for Da Costa, because that crook no longer exists for me, and should I happen to run across him, I will greet the bastard politely. I feel that he's still around, but I'm not wandering about Victoria and Kowloon to provoke a confrontation. That man is evil, and that's quite all right by me. Evil, anyway, is no more than a dualistic concept that makes no sense because reality is above, or underneath, all contradiction.

Chinese, Syben thought, are known for their cleanliness, but the Chinese of this neighborhood have to be exceptions because they throw garbage into their streets and waterways. Exotic? Yes. Smelly? That too.

This is, Syben thought, where I enter the colony's shadow side. He wanted to turn back but became fascinated by the dark and fetid environment. Houses and stores had crumbled and faded from neglect; mold, sponge moss, even full-grown weeds growing from refuse stuffed in gutters, made the multiple roofs of a nearby pagoda sag. The ever-present sampans he had seen so far were, even when simply designed and crafted, pleasant to behold, but here a murky waterscape was

dotted with wrecked boats, barely afloat, built up with anything that might keep hostile elements out for a while: lopsided tents of torn material, flapping plastic sheeting, soggy
cartons. Bigger structures consisted of rusty bus bodies on
junked ferries, rotten plank roofs tottering above an aban-
doned tugboat's dented hull.

A dead upside-down dog, short legs reaching up in stiff
despair from a hugely bloated body, was pushed smartly out
of the way by a long gleaming oar. Syben, about to turn
away to walk back to more cheerful parts of the city, stared
at the rower. "No," Syben whispered, but the man in the
rapidly approaching dory, most likely on his way from a
vessel moored further out to sea, undoubtedly was Da Costa,
impeccable in his shantung suit and wide-brimmed straw hat.
He turned the small boat, backing it to the quay, while he
reached for a rope neatly rolled under his seat, to throw to a
man ashore.

Syben smiled his welcome, held out a helpful hand. He
looked impeccable, too, in his fine light-colored Manhattan
summer suit, with his long golden hair brushed down on his
wide shoulders. I'm a good guy, Syben thought, and so he
might be. The sun's rays confirmed the image by suddenly
sliding through a crack in clouds, so that they could complete
this majestic figure with a radiant aura, while Da Costa's
dory floated into dark shadows, cast by the seawall looming
ahead. Bad guy leers upward into the blinding light; good
guy stares down into the gloomy dark. Good and suitable
imagery, Syben thought, changing Da Costa into a devil
cowering below in filth (the dory was surrounded by a mattress and other decaying matter floating in black oil), himself
into a revenging angel, invincible, poised on a shiny cloud.

"Good evening, Mr. Da Costa," Syben said coldly but
kindly, ready to catch the rope, pull in his rightful prey,
dispose of the evil symbol by proper use of martial arts.

Da Costa dropped the rope. "Good evening, Mr. Sobryne."
He picked up his oars, pulled, made the dory shoot off with
long, strong strokes.

Good wins in the end, so evil loses. Backed up by this

simple reasoning, Syben dived, swam with long, strong strokes, not very far, for the decomposing mattress entangled him, oil got into his eyes, and while he struggled to escape from the choking slime and debris that pulled him down, he hit his head sharply against a submerged metal object. Syben Sobryne fainted, then peacefully began to drown.

"He was saved by a gentleman in a dory," the doctor said. "The ambulance driver reported that the gentleman saw him slip off the quay, dragged him out, called us, and was with him when the ambulance arrived. The gentleman had urgent business and had to go then, but he phoned here to inquire, just a few minutes ago. His name is Da Costa. He was pleased to hear that Mr. Sobryne's wound isn't serious and sends his best wishes."

"Can we take my brother with us?" Mark asked.

"As soon as you pay his bill," the doctor said. "The water near Hung Hom is dirty, but we took extra care. There should be no infection. A few days' rest and he will be fine."

"Da Costa!" Little Giant shouted. "Let's get him. Where's the phone? Are the police good here?"

"What?" the doctor asked.

"A thief!" Little Giant shouted. "He filched my stamps."

"He saved your brother's life," the doctor said.

Little Giant looked through the Chinese characters in the Chinese telephone book. "Where's *P* in Chinese?"

The doctor was called away.

Mathilde stroked Syben's tar-stained hair. "You ruined your suit, too."

"Add it to the bill," Mark said. "One soggy suit. Did Da Costa throw you into the harbor?"

"I dived in," Syben said. "Did you book the trip home yet?"

Little Giant dropped the telephone book. He dialed *0*. The telephone hummed softly. "Operator?" Little Giant shouted.

"We go tomorrow," Mark said, "but I'll cancel. Maybe Da Costa can be caught."

"Let it ride," Syben said. "Maybe I learned something; maybe I'll learn later what it was." He smiled at Mathilde. "How're you doing? All recovered?"

She helped him get up. "Much better, thank you. Da Costa looked through me. I'm not strong enough for that type of man."

"Hey! Hey!" Little Giant shouted.

Mark tugged gently at the phone.

"Let it go, dear," Mathilde said.

Syben nodded. "Yes. Do it. Go on." He caught the phone when Little Giant dropped it.

The doctor came back with the bill. Little Giant paid. He muttered during the cab ride back.

"What's that?" Mark asked.

Little Giant crooked a finger, closed one eye.

Mark raised an eyebrow.

"Come closer," Little Giant whispered. Mark leaned over. "Did you and Mathilde. . . ?" Little Giant whispered into Mark's ear.

"Did what?" Mark asked.

"No, we didn't," Mathilde said. "I was too ill and Mark too nice."

"Good," Little Giant said. "If you had, I would have complained with the goddess Tyen Hou."

Tyen Hou helped them to have a safe journey home. Nothing happened except that Syben found a yo-yo forgotten by a child in Kai Tak Airport. Syben yo-yoed in the plane until the stewardess stopped him after she stumbled over the string.

ROTTERDAM
AGAIN

CHAPTER 25

MATHILDE switched the lights on and the television's sound off. She poured tea.

Syben played with his yo-yo. Mark and Little Giant kept on watching the TV, which showed a girl gasping for air while being silently manhandled by a quiet intruder whose lopsided grin suggested sadistic intentions.

Syben caught his yo-yo again. "I know what you're going to say now, Mathilde."

"That I am so happy in the midst of you three." Mathilde said.

"And that this reminds you of the many pleasant evenings with Dad."

"And so it does," Mathilde said.

Mark turned off the set. "But Dad's apartment was better-looking than this ill-assorted agglomeration of bad taste. I never used to see my home like that, but now the ugliness oppresses me. It reminds me of Geraldine, and myself, mostly."

"So what would you rather have?" Little Giant asked.

"Dad's apartment."

Syben's yo-yo zipped up, jumped off its string, touched his muscular right arm, ricocheted, and returned to the string. "Do you know what that costs?"

Mark waved the newspaper. "Less than what we sold it for."

"The apartment is listed?"

"It certainly is."

Syben whistled. "How much less?"

"A third."

"That's still far too high for you," Syben said.

"Every cent is too much," Mark said, "because I'm broke, but Little Giant asked what I wanted, and I want to live in Dad's apartment."

"With Mathilde, I suppose," Little Giant said.

"Yes," Mark said.

"Shouldn't you ask me?" Mathilde asked. "Maybe I don't want to live with you in your dad's apartment."

Little Giant winked. "Of course you do. Luxurious surroundings that fit your style of life, an uninterrupted view of the Kralingen Lake bordered by woods, and Mark seems to be quite nice these days."

"That's true," Mathilde said. "But my career as companion lady is over. I want to study art history and work for a museum after I get my degree."

"And Mark has no money," Syben said.

Mark drank his tea. "And no job, but I will get one again. All this journeying has awakened me. I see possibilities again."

Syben got up and made the yo-yo zoom under his arm. "Then you'll have to wait for a while because our collective effort continues. It's my turn now to attempt an increase of our capital remnants. The game won't be over until I say so."

"When your money is used, too," Little Giant said. "That's what you mean, and you have no grasp on the duration. Neither had we. Suddenly it's all gone, and you're watching the horizon with your mouth open."

"Your mouth is closed," Syben said. "And you have been able to save a good part."

"Do you have a plan?" Mark asked.

"Yo-yos."

"Where is the East?" Little Giant asked.

"Where the sun rises," Mathilde said, "in the rear room, where the begonias are."

Little Giant walked into the rear room.

"What is he going to do?" Mark asked.

"Pray," Syben said. "He's got some connection with a Chinese goddess. Let him be. I can explain my plan without him. Yo-yos are an article of fashion."

"Not right now," Mark said. "The only one who is playing with a yo-yo is you, and I wish you would stop it. That zipping and zooming is beginning to irritate me a little."

"Yes, please, not just now, Syben," Mathilde said.

Syben plucked the yo-yo from the air and put it into his pocket. "Yo-yos are the rage, and the rage will suddenly erupt. Every generation forgets the yo-yo, and the next one rediscovers it. The time of rediscovering the yo-yo is now."

"Do you see that in your deeper meditations?" Mark asked.

"I see it when I walk in the street," Syben said. "The neighbor's little sons come after me to ask where they can buy yo-yos."

"Yes," Mathilde said, "they rang the bell this morning. They made me go all the way downstairs just to tell them I didn't know."

Mathilde raised the teapot. Syben held up his cup. "So, it's quite simple. We are the only ones to know that there is a demand for yo-yos. There are no regular suppliers of yo-yos; all we have to do is find a manufacturer, which I have already done."

"Expensive?" Mark asked.

"Mr. Knaaps, whose shop is in the Second Meuse Alley, owns modern woodworking machines and happens to have little to do at this time. He's prepared to sign a statement that he will supply no yo-yos except to us for half a year if we give him an order for fifty thousand. Between the cost price, inclusive of string and a lovely box that the printer Verberg will be delighted to supply, and the selling price, some profit is hidden."

"That's nice," Mark said, "and how much would that profit be?"

"I multiplied by two."

"You are the wholesaler. What will the retailer ask for the product?"

"He will multiply by two as well and sell at eight."

"Eight guilders for a yo-yo?" Mathilde asked. "Isn't that far too expensive? And why does everybody multiply by two?"

"That's the customary figure," Mark said. "Two is the factor of prosperity, of the continuing exhaustion of raw materials, of pollution, of atomic weapons, of the rush to the end. While we double . . ."

"It's the figure of hashish," Syben said, "of corporation A that was going to fuse with corporation B, of the pigskins, of the cocoa beans, of the postage stamps, of the—"

"Yo-yos," Mark said.

"Yes," Syben said, "and I spoke to the buyer of a well-known chain of department stores, the central buyer for the entire country, and that gentleman, whose name is Boarish and who is, to all appearances, a man who moves on high levels. Mr. Boarish says that he's willing to buy fifty thousand yo-yos, with a three percent cash discount for payment within ten days and a period of exclusivity of a month and a half."

"Mr. Boarish is crazy," Mark said. "Why doesn't he have the yo-yos manufactured himself?"

Syben sat down again. "He is not crazy, and he believes me."

"You're wearing a new suit," Mathilde said. "A blue suit with thin white stripes, and a waistcoat, just like your father had."

"Turn your head," Mark said.

Syben looked at the wall.

"You cut off your ponytail."

"Oh, Syben," Mathilde said. "Is that why you came in so quietly and hid in that dark corner? Poor Syben, but I think you look even more handsome now."

"This is not the time to make compliments," Mark said, "this is the time to do business. So what did Mr. Boarish believe?"

"That I am the owner of Sobryne Incorporated and that there are fifty thousand yo-yos in our warehouse ready for distribution. He also believes that I, an experienced entrepreneur, am ready to start a national campaign in order to demonstrate and advertise the yo-yo game."

"You have a signed purchase order?" Mark asked.

Syben put the paper on the table.

"And the box?"

Syben got up, brought in an attaché case from the corridor, and showed the box. "This is only a prototype, put together and lettered by hand."

"Good box," Little Giant said.

"I thought you were praying," Syben said.

"I never pray for long. That's a most attractive box. Slick drawing, fresh colors, inviting lettering, very salable. I'm with you."

"So am I," Mark said. "Yo-yo championships. A TV commentator playing with a yo-yo while he performs. Slides in the cinema before the movie starts. Yo-yos as therapeutic relaxation for conveyer-belt laborers. Practical joy, and sales in multiples of a hundred thousand. The Common Market is open; America will be next."

"Ach, Mark," Mathilde said.

Mark nibbled on his cookie. "I was only joking, Mathilde, but the idea is sound, and a little enthusiasm while we start the campaign can't do any harm. I know, of course, that if the woodworker Knaaps on the Second Meuse Alley can manufacture yo-yos . . ."

Little Giant jumped up. "Can't we manufacture them ourselves? It'll save a lot of money. Nothing to it. You take a four-foot log, like this, and you attach it, here, and on the other side, like that, and you make it turn, *rom-rom-rom*, and you adjust your knives, here and here and here, and you slice the lot in pieces, *wop-wop-wop*, and then you insert a new log, like this and . . ."

"Easy, now," Mark said. "Sit down, there's a good fellow. Mathilde, pour him another cup of tea. Drop in a sleeping tablet; he's used to it."

"We should never touch the manufacturing side of our product," Syben said, "and Mark is right. If Mr. Knaaps can make them, so can others. There'll be an untold number of woodworkers in the country. All we have to do is get in first, and get out again before it's all over. Not too late, but not too early, either. We'll have to stop at the right moment."

"Slides?" Little Giant asked. "Why not a short movie? Now, if Syben would teach Mathilde to play yo-yo, Mathilde or some other good looking broad—but another broad will cost money."

"I used to be good at playing handball," Mathilde said.

"Mathilde is no broad," Mark said.

"In a miniskirt," Little Giant said, "and in high heels and a wet T-shirt, or topless, perhaps . . ."

"Some more tea, Little Giant?" Mathilde asked.

"Don't pour it down his neck," Syben said.

"I wasn't altogether serious," Little Giant said, "but just a little topless, perhaps?"

"Would you like the tea on your head?"

"In my cup," Little Giant said. "And if you don't want to cooperate, you don't have to."

"I'd love to cooperate."

"Forward march," Syben said.

CHAPTER 26

LITTLE Giant brushed his teeth at the washstand. Mark was in the bathtub reading the paper. "Dad's apartment is being advertised again—for even less money. Our client seems to be in urgent need of getting rid of the property."

Little Giant stopped brushing his teeth. "Do you really want to buy the apartment?"

"Yes, and I could have bought it before everything began to go wrong."

Little Giant spat and looked at the mirror. "But now everything is going right again. How many yo-yos have we sold so far?"

"A hundred thousand."

"And how many more do we have to deliver?"

"Twenty thousand, but Mr. Knaaps is having troubles. He can't keep up, even if he's working day and night, and we can't go to another woodworker because of our contract."

Little Giant sat on the edge of the tub. "The competition is nowhere."

Mark splashed in the bath foam. "You can't know that."

"I can, because I've been around. Nobody else can manufacture yo-yos in such large quantities and so quickly."

"Turn a four-foot log, *wop-wop-wop*," Mark said.

Little Giant combed his hair. "And that short movie is doing very well; it's showing in all the cinemas."

"At our expense," Mark said, "and we keep on paying. I wonder if it's got anything to do with the sales?"

Little Giant pulled the plug out of the bath.

"Now what are you doing?"

"You have to get out," Little Giant said.

"Why?"

"Because I have to get in," Little Giant said. "And Mathilde's good with that yo-yo, don't you think? I've seen that movie ten times at least, and I keep applauding, especially at the part where the yo-yo slips along her breasts. She should have been topless."

Mark grabbed a towel. "I think that that idea is terrible. How can you prostitute your own father's mistress?"

Little Giant filled the bath again. "The public doesn't know that. The public is a faceless mass buying yo-yos."

Mark dried himself. "I tell you that you're making a lowly profit out of a noble woman, and I do not appreciate your dirty talk."

Little Giant stepped into the bath. "You're talking nonsense, Mark. That goddess in Hong Kong was a noble woman because she answered my prayer, but she also had a cleavage, and not a little one, either, and flowing thighs, very visible in the slits of her skirt."

Mark grabbed a faucet. "I believe that you want cold water in the tub."

"If you open that tap I will not tell you how Dad got hold of Mathilde."

The cold water splashed into the foam, and Little Giant shrieked.

"First dirty talk," Mark said, "and now filthy lies. A cold bath will elevate your thoughts."

Mathilde opened the door and peered through the crack. "Don't tease your brother, Mark. There'll be coffee when you're ready."

"Pass the soap," Little Giant said.

"You are a fiend," Mark snapped.

"No, I'm a dwarf. Now, do you want to hear how Dad met Mathilde?"

"First tell me how you penetrated the secret."

Little Giant spread out his wet beard. "I am a dwarf, right? Dwarfs obtain their information from another angle. Because they're small, they seem to be helpless, so the big people want to protect them and trust their innocence. When a lovely giantess like Mathilde is washing the dishes and a dwarf like me is standing next to her on a stool and dries the dishes, then an intimate contact may form. The giantess talks easily, and the dwarf listens attentively."

"And then the dwarf runs about and tells everybody."

"Not everybody, only his older brother, and he communicates his exclusive knowledge with the very best intentions. There is a difference between gossip mongering and supplying useful information."

"Now, tell your tale," Mark said, "to get it out of the way."

"Mathilde was married to a gangster."

"A despicable cad."

"Yes."

"Who was shot to death on a French beach."

"Yes, but by that time Mathilde had left him already. She steered an unsteady course through Amsterdam, and had no money, and lived in a room with the wallpaper peeling off."

"And ate jam from a jar."

"With her fingers," Little Giant said. "She had found that jar in a cupboard, and there was a thick layer of mold on the strawberry jelly that she had to get through first."

"With her fingers."

"A sad situation," Little Giant said, "that could not be allowed to last. She had to have money, and if she asked for help, everybody would immediately abuse her. You know what we are like."

Mark took a handful of foam from the bath and blew it away. "I know it, but we also have our good sides."

"But those will only appear after we have been punished cruelly by the consequences of our own mistakes, and even then we will lay our grabbing hands on a defenseless and lovely lady who humbly approaches us to ask for a sandwich."

"We certainly will," Mark said.

"So," Little Giant said, "Mathilde, who is lovely but not exactly stupid, decided that she would beat fate to the punch."

Mark reached for the cold tap. "I don't want to hear it. She is going to throw herself away. She will allow puffy hands covered with flashy diamonds to smudge her innocence forever. She has to degrade herself in private, perhaps even in public. Maybe all of this has happened, just like the mold that she dug from her jam jar. Yes, it probably really happened, but I don't have to know." Mark turned the faucet.

"Belay," Little Giant said, "or I'll scream again."

Mark closed the tap.

"So," Little Giant said, "our Mathilde applies some makeup, possible because she still owned her handbag, and set out for an expensive hotel."

"I'm going to have my coffee," Mark said.

"You will stay right here," Little Giant said, "because you're much too curious not to hear how Dad behaved."

Mark tried to stare Little Giant down. "Listen here, everybody needs certain examples, images that he invokes when things go wrong, beloved shapes to which he turns for support and comfort. I don't know how you think about Dad, but for me he remains a pure, dear figure, and if you are going to strip off his veneer, you will cut off my last escape. And Mathilde is a noble lady. If you are crazy enough to pray to a goddess with funny eyes . . ."

"Keep your hands off Tyen Hou," Little Giant shouted.

"Exactly," Mark said, "so let me kneel at Mathilde's feet."

"Kneel as much as you like."

"Then keep your story to yourself."

"No," Little Giant said, "because you are my older brother, and I have too much respect for you to hide the truth. In her radiant innocence Mathilde entered that hotel while tortured by hunger pangs and climbed on a bar stool. She ordered a glass of cola and waited for her prey."

Mark shivered.

"Mathilde as a *femme fatale*, as a vamp, as a barfly, as a tart of pleasure—and she's such a nice girl, really, right Mark? We did get to know her well enough."

"And then Dad walked into that bar?" Mark asked.

"Yes. And what was Dad doing in Amsterdam anyway? He lived in Rotterdam."

"The view of the Kralingen Lake and its wooded shores might have gotten too much for him."

"No," Little Giant said, "there is nothing wrong with that expensive view, and when we have finished with the yo-yos, I do advise you to buy that apartment back. Dad happened to feel lonely, and in Amsterdam one can talk to strangers without the strangers thinking that you want to abuse their company. Dad walked to the bar and sat down, two stools away from Mathilde."

"Who made the first move? Surely not Dad. His manners were always impeccable."

"Dad made the move after Mathilde had wished him a good evening."

Mark got up again. "Enough. Dad follows Mathilde up the stairs. Her slender ankles make him lustful. He eyes her long legs lasciviously. He thinks in the most common terms of the gutter. He imagines, crudely, how he will misbehave. Then he does misbehave, a few minutes later, after she has summoned him to make an appreciable cash payment. Dad . . ."

"Whatever makes you think that?" Little Giant asked. "Why are you forcing your own vile thoughts into Dad's civilized brain? Dad didn't do any of all that. He invited Mathilde out to dinner."

"And that was it?"

"After dinner he took her home to Kralingen."

"Nothing more?"

"Well," Little Giant said, "Dad and Mathilde did live together for three years. Something might have happened afterward. Mathilde might have made a ring of rice one night and filled up the center with a ragout of veal, and served mocha mousse afterward, and Dad might have opened a bottle of a respectably old wine. Candlelight. A full moon above the Kralinger Lake and . . ."

". . . and its wooded shores," Mark said. "Eroticism doesn't always have to be dirty."

Mark and Little Giant walked into the living room together. "That wasn't too bad, was it?" Little Giant asked. Mark put his arm around Little Giant's shoulder.

"I thought you two were fighting," Mathilde said. "Syben just phoned. He's coming home and wants to discuss business."

"Listen here," Syben said, "the yo-yo madness is going full blast, but Mr. Knaaps does not want to sell to us anymore. He has a weak heart, he said, and money isn't everything."

"So we find another woodworker," Mark said.

"The other woodworker is a fully automated factory, and the director sports a shark's head. He'll fill our order, but only if we sign for a hundred thousand yo-yos and pay in advance. His price is higher than that of Mr. Knaaps."

"Let's go ahead," Little Giant said. "Don't you think? One last fling?"

"We have multiplied our capital," Mark said, "and the operation is still profitable. We can order two hundred thousand if Mr. Sharkhead wishes us to do so, and then we may wish his price to go down."

"Ach, Mark," Mathilde said.

"I wasn't saying anything," Mark said. "I was thinking aloud."

"Who will make the decision?" Syben asked.

"You," Mark said.

Syben looked at Mathilde.

"You," Mathilde said.

"You," Little Giant said. "We have lost our chances, and we have all reached the point at which you now are. You're in unsteady balance, but perhaps you'll fall to the side of the safe feeling."

"I need a few hours of peace,' Syben said.

"Finish your coffee first," Mark said, "and then go to the little room in the loft. Nobody will disturb you there."

"And some attributes," Syben said, "like cushions and incense."

"Take the cushions from the couch," Mathilde said, "and there is a Chinese store at the corner."

CHAPTER 27

SWEETLY perfumed smoke crinkled toward the hardboard paneling of the low slanting roof. Ash crumbled and dropped into the sand-filled copper bowl between Syben's cushions and the wainscoting under the windowsill. Syben sat motionless, back stretched, legs tucked into each other. His eyes were closed, but had he been able to see, he would have seen the soles of his own feet. Next to him lay a page from a notebook on which he had, vaguely disturbed by the bells of passing streetcars along the boulevard outside, noted his calculations. At that time he'd still been thinking, in illuminated figures that flashed through his brain. Now there were no thoughts. The figure on the last line of the notepaper expressed a considerable amount, the total of invested capital plus profit.

That figure had started his ruminations, but by now he had forgotten what it was.

Syben had sat for some time. Darkness slid into the room.

New images began to appear. The images were complicated and indistinct. The designs kept changing and eventually merged into a single shape, built of different parts. Da Costa had old Sobryne's face and Mathilde's legs. Little Giant had the face of the goddess Tyen Hou and Mark's once prominent belly. Mark had Van Putte's face and Syben's former ponytail. The kaleidoscopic figure's behavior kept changing, too. The phenomenon was offering Syben noodle soup, in a sampan floating on the pond of New York's Rockefeller Center. The next moment it had Saud's face and saved Syben from a yo-yo manufacturing shark's mouth. The projections didn't bubble up from recent times only, for the shape also absorbed aspects that belonged to his guru, at the feet of the Himalayas, and to the mercenary sergeant from Chad.

Syben's calves cramped, and he untwisted his legs and shuffled on his knees to the bowl to light incense. He sat down again. The shape reappeared and threatened him.

I am beyond fear, Syben thought as he became frightened.

The shape shamed Syben's faith by crooking him in many ways, from crude to hardly noticeable. I am beyond all anger, Syben thought, and became quite angry.

He fought the enemy but unsuccessfully, because the shape changed once again and became Mathilde surrounded by painted backdrops that imitated his Manhattan hotel room's interior quite cleverly.

Yes, Syben thought, to sit here in Mark's loft behind an erection doesn't serve much purpose.

He wanted to leave, to go downstairs to the Javanese rice that Mathilde was cooking, which sent delicious fragrances that stole up the stairs, but he wasn't finished yet, though the shape had again changed it components and was supplying answers to questions that Syben could formulate clearly.

All sorts of interesting information was given free of charge, and the meditator watched amused while the shape demonstrated how Mark would continue on his way, and what would happen to Little Giant, and how Mathilde fit into the future. Syben understood now who old Sobryne had really been, and saw his father's ideals and how vague they were, but how right nevertheless.

Mathilde came into the room and put down a plate of fried rice and a thermos flask of tea. She left again. Syben left too for a few moments, to go to the toilet.

Evening changed into night. Syben hardly moved. The incense smoldered.

The morning light touched the window sill and drew a line on the paneling. Syben heard the others get up and move about in the bathroom. He left the loft.

"Welcome," Little Giant said. "We weren't quite expecting you yet, but you can have my egg."

"And. . . ?" Mathilde poured coffee.

"And. . . ?" Mark asked.

"And what?"

"The yo-yos?"

"The what?"

"That's impossible," Little Giant said. "You can't have forgotten the yo-yos. I don't mind if you want to make us believe that you have reached higher spheres, but you shouldn't exaggerate. The yo-yos, right?"

"Let him have his coffee first," Mathilde said.

CHAPTER 28

"No," Syben said, "I think we should forget the yo-yos."

"Very well," Mark said.

"Oh my God," Mathilde said. "I'm so pleased."

"No more yo-yos," Little Giant said. "Now what?"

"As far as I'm concerned," Syben said, "we're all done. And I want to leave you, too, because I've got other things to do. Let's share the yo-yo money."

"Plus what's left of my share," Little Giant said. "Can I have the top of your egg? All of one egg may be too much for you after your recent spiritualization."

Syben passed the top of his egg.

"You can keep your pennies," Mark said, "because Mathilde and I really have no right to speak."

Little Giant scratched his eggshell. Syben felt his bristly chin.

"Yes or no?"

"No," Syben said.

"No," Little Giant said. "Greed, in the intimacy of the family, is a waste of effort, but we're still short a million."

"Which million?" Syben asked.

"There he goes again," Little Giant said.

"Which million?" Mark asked. "You know anything about a million, Mathilde?"

"I don't know anything. All I know is that Syben is now providing four hundred thousand and Little Giant fifty."

"Are you serious?" Little Giant asked. "Or are you teasing a retarded dwarf?"

"You're not really retarded," Mark said, "and even if

you were, you'd still be well off with one-fourth of the loot."

"Buy some bonds," Little Giant said, "or something else that's quite safe. I want to get back to my cottage on the dike and weave strange shapes. I don't think I'm in need of any money. All I can think of is that my junker could do with a new muffler."

"Bonds aren't safe anymore," Mark said. "I'm going to buy Dad's apartment back."

"For a hundred thousand?"

Mark shook the newspaper. "The price keeps coming down, and I'll risk a counter offer, with a mortgage for the difference."

"You want to live by yourself in all that space?"

"I want to marry Mathilde."

"Then you'll have to ask for my hand," Mathilde said.

Mark got up, crossed his chest with his right arm, bowed and asked if Mathilde would like to marry him.

"Yes," Mathilde said.

"So that's taken care of," Little Giant said. "Did you manage to get a job?"

"Yes," Mark said, "with a mutual fund company. I told them that I've just returned from an investigation of the Far East and that I've also spent some time checking figures in America. I can start next month in an assistant position and will be required to contemplate distant possibilities."

"Oh my God," Mathilde said.

Mark bowed again. "Experience has taught me that the greatest care will be required, and I promise you that my advice will not only be solid but also . . ."

"That's not what I mean. You'll be gone all the time."

"But he'll be coming back all the time, too," Syben said, "and you've got to study. Art history, do you remember? And later on, suitable employment in a museum?"

"You can always travel with me," Mark said. "How can I love you when you're not around?"

"And I . . ." Syben said.

"I'll tell you what you'll do," Little Giant said. "You'll grow your hair again and dress in jeans and an aviator jacket.

You'll buy a Harley-Davidson and disappear across the horizon."

"How do you know?"

'True or not?"

"True," Syben said.

Little Giant studied his empty eggshell. "I don't have to play holy all night in order to foresee the future. If one frames one's questions in the way Syben seems to think is necessary, the answers will not be found in Rotterdam." He crushed his eggshell with his fist. "Although the answers *can* be found in Rotterdam, of course."

Mark sat down. "Then we have reached our temporary goal, with the exception of sharing the money and celebrating the marriage."

"Shouldn't you be kissing Mathilde or something?" Syben asked.

Mathilde rummaged in her handbag. "In a minute. Here." She held up a cassette. "Can we play this on your recorder, Mark?"

"What's on it?" Little Giant asked.

"Your father's voice."

"But haven't we listened to that tape already?"

"Not this one," Mathilde answered. "Your father asked me to play it at the right moment, but I never knew what moment he could have meant. I think he meant now. Don't you think so?"

CHAPTER 29

THE TAPE hissed.

"Hello, my sons," old Mr. Sobryne said. "Hello, dear Mathilde. I recorded this tape alone and made Mathilde promise not to play it before, because I meant to surprise her, too."

A click. Sucking sounds.

"What's he doing now?" Little Giant asked.

"He's lighting a small cigar," Mathilde said.

"Yes," old Mr. Sobryne said, "and now I'm even further away from you, because I've been dead for quite a while. A most extraordinary thought. I can't get used to it. What I have to tell you could possibly be complete nonsense, because who am I to foresee the future? But I thought, and think, that you're not together in order to divide what's left of the million that remained."

Mark jumped up and pushed the recorder's button. "So he *knew*, the old fox."

"Push that button again," Syben said.

"You must have been gambling somehow," old Sobryne said. "It couldn't be otherwise. Half the inheritance suddenly disappears, and a lost half makes a big hole, but the remaining half gave you a chance to make good."

The tape hissed.

"Or am I wrong?" old Sobryne asked. "My manipulation didn't cause any difficulties, did it? I didn't expect too much trouble because Mathilde was there. She is a good influence. She always stopped me from going on in a childish manner. Beauty and a positive discipline are connected somehow." Pause. "Heh heh."

"He's laughing at us," Little Giant said.

"I shouldn't be laughing at you," Sobryne said, "because what you did, I should have done. A man should take a chance once in a while, and I never dared. Because you are my continuation, my fault may be overcome; no story ever ends. That's to say . . ."

"Hello?" Little Giant asked.

"I beg your pardon," old Sobryne said. "I had to think for a moment. The existence of someone who leaves no children also continues, in the consequences of his deeds. I shouldn't overstate my position as a father. By the way, may I thank the person who was kind enough to make that one million disappear? I hope that person succeeded so well that she or he was not exclusively suspected by the others, because that would have destroyed your mutual relationship. Was the party a success? I do hope that Mathilde has been able to contain the sex element that belongs to that type of merry-making. She's quite a woman, but the timidity that I always showed on such occasions must have rubbed off on my sons, and some sense of common decency . . . hmm."

"Don't worry Dad," Little Giant said.

"*You* should say that," Mark said.

"Not that I wouldn't grant you certain favors," old Mr. Sobryne said, "and if Mathilde in her goodness . . ."

"Quite so," Mathilde said.

"But enough of this," old Sobryne said. "I know that times have changed, and timidity may not be an admirable quality anymore. It's quite acceptable these days to exercise some sexual freedom—*echrem*—" Old Sobryne cleared his throat.

The tape hissed.

"I'm just jealous. How silly, considering that I'm dead. Quite ridiculous. What do I care? Do as you like and have a good time. About the money, now. The million that seemed to disappear is still available."

"As if I didn't know," Syben said. "Of course it's still available. Where is it, Dad?"

"Deposited in a solid and most reliable mutual fund that has served its members for over fifty years. If somebody will fetch a ballpoint, I will dictate the name of the fund and your account number."

Mark made a note.

"Mark?"

"Yes?" Mark asked.

"I still have a few words for you."

Mark stopped the machine. He waited until the others had left the room, turned the recorder's volume down and started it again.

"I think," old Sobryne said, "that one of you should marry Mathilde. She won't mind marrying you. You're a bit of a windbag, but I imagine that you will have lost some of your egocentricity by now. I know you were fired because I was told by one of your bosses, the same acquaintance whom I introduced you to after you received your Ph.D. A man who suddenly loses his job has an excellent opportunity to learn, and the trouble with Geraldine will have woken you up too."

"Do carry on," Mark said.

"I know that you can't defend yourself and that this may hurt you, but you're alone while you're listening to me, and I expect you to destroy the tape when I'm done. Little Giant could make a good husband for Mathilde, too. I'm also rather small-sized. . . ."

The tape hissed.

"I was rather small-sized," Mr. Sobryne said. "I can't get used to being dead. When you hear this, I will have no size at all. Hard to believe. How can a man disappear altogether? He does, however."

"Little Giant is undersized," old Sobryne continued, "but that shouldn't affect the possibility of a happy marriage. A physical shortcoming may even provoke protective feelings from the partner. Besides, Little Giant is quite amusing. He has realized relativity much better than I."

"*I* will marry Mathilde," Mark said, "not Little Giant."

"And Syben," old Sobryne said. "Wouldn't Mathilde and Syben be a lovely couple? Both so good looking?"

"Syben is no good for marriage," Mark said.

"Syben may not have time to marry yet," old Sobryne

said. "He should keep going his own way, perhaps. Syben is my question, my wonder, my admiration for everything that's alive, that exists. Admiration by itself, though, is not enough. Syben's hectic movements used to annoy me, because I thought a man should aim for a certain goal. I always attempted to live according to the national ideal. I always tried to be thoughtful, diligent, to work dutifully for . . . for what? And isn't Syben doing that, too? In his own way? I hope he doesn't stay here," old Sobryne said.

"He isn't staying. He'll be riding off on his motorcycle, destination unknown." Mark looked out of the window. "And it's raining again. He'll have to wear a yellow plastic suit, and waterproof boots that'll fill up anyway. Bah, not my game at all."

"The great game," old Sobryne said, "but the boy should have some base. If Syben leaves the money where it is now, his capital will probaby increase, keep up with inflation anyway, so that he may wander about in peace. Surely I can do that much for him."

"I won't let him stay with me," Mark said, "because he'll get at Mathilde."

"Mathilde is a faithful woman," Sobryne said, "and she'll love her squire. She thought I was her squire. She'll think the same of you."

Mark bowed his head.

"I'm dizzy again," old Sobryne said, "really quite a wonderful feeling. I'm looking at the wallpaper, Mark, and the lines keep moving; they disappear into the ceiling and slide up again from the floor. From nothing to nothing. Luminous lines . . ."

There was nothing more on the tape.

"You can come in now," Mark called.

"Your father died after he rewound that tape," Mathilde said. "He was very happy and contented."

No story ever ends, because events keep connecting, whether according to expectations or not.

Mark married Mathilde. The couple now lives in the

Kralingen apartment, once a substantial part of Mark's father's estate. Mark bought it back from it's new owner, smartly, at half price. No need to pity the losing party. The man was no good and had used the elegant address as a front for shady business. He got into trouble with ruthless partners, needed cash . . . Mark stepped in.

Mathilde began her studies at the university. She gets good grades.

Little Giant had his cottage remodeled and his old car repaired. He continues weaving baskets but now also creates female forms, using a technique seen in Tunisia. His shapes are both sensuous and bizarre and fetch good prices. Trendy galleries regularly show his work.

Syben disappeared but may drop in again. His last postcard was stamped in Lhasa, Tibet.

The person who deposited the "lost" million in the name of all heirs wasn't identified for a while.

He must have just taken the money while the others slept, let himself out, and hid it . . . where?

In a car, parked behind the building? Probably. Who expects to find a million guilders pushed under a seat, or in the trunk, under the spare wheel? Maybe even under the hood, next to the battery, perhaps.

So who?

Mathilde denied it, Mark wouldn't confess, Little Giant smirked, and Syben refused to discuss the matter.

The question was answered, finally, after a dinner celebrating Mark and Mathilde's wedding.

"Well?" Little Giant asked.

"Well what?" Mark asked.

"This may irritate the company," Little Giant said, "as it did before, but who took Dad's million?"

There were moments of silence.

"You really don't know?" Mathilde asked Little Giant.

"He just wants to know that we know," Syben said.

"Little Giant," Mark said, "don't look baffled."

"Me?" Little Giant asked.

Syben smirked. Mark asked the waiter for four napkins and four ballpoints.

The waiter, who hadn't yet been paid, was quick to oblige.

Mark thanked him. "Now, everyone, please write down the name of our beloved thief. Then we fold the napkins, Mathilde shuffles and unfolds. How's that?"

Everyone wrote.

Mathilde shuffled.

Syben read. "Little Giant . . . Little Giant . . . Me . . . Little Giant."

"No," Little Giant said. "No shit. Excuse me, Mathilde. You all knew?"

"Not right away," Mark said. "The truth dawned gradually. You did a good job."

"I knew it," Syben said, "most of the time. Who else would have done it?" He grinned. "But you did well."

"I knew all the time," Mathilde said. "Dear Little Giant. Never underestimate a sober woman. Do you recall that I didn't drink either that night?"

"I acted drunk," Little Giant said. "I'm a good actor. I didn't convince you?"

"With clear eyes?" Syben asked. "Maybe I didn't see that your eyes weren't bloodshot, because I was drunk, but Mathilde must have noticed. I saw that you brought in your own genever. I remembered that you don't particularly care for Dutch gin. Besides, you were never known to indulge."

Little Giant shrugged. "I got drunk in the Sahara."

Mark shrugged, too. "Of course. We all suffered shell shock then."

"So?" Little Giant asked. "Dad died, that was a shock, too, good reason to get drunk."

"Yes," Syben said, "but you brought your own bottle, filled with water, I'm sure. At parties you usually have one whiskey. You managed to take mine. Mark and I got smashed. Drunks are boring. You wanted to be a little bit tipsy, too, to put up with our blabbing, but you made quite sure not to get drunk."

"Remember," Mathilde asked, "that I said that your father

made tapes? Tapes, plural? I only played one. There was another, so I thought your dad might have a surprise for us all. I would have to play the surprise tape at the right moment. The right moment would, I imagined correctly, come when we had finished playing with the leftover million. I was sure your father left orders with Brother X for safe investment of the missing million. Now, who else could Brother X be but you?"

"Indeed," Mark said. "Listen. Dad loved Mathilde more than any of us, trusted her more, too, I'm sure, but he couldn't let her take the money. Just think what we would have done to the poor lady if we had caught her in the act?"

"Or to me?" Syben said. "I'm family, of course, but I never fit in. I'm unable to live the acceptable Dutch life. I never even dared to get on the straight and narrow. When Dad made up his will, I was out of a job, looked like a hippie, lived in a loft. You might have thought I was a junkie."

"You'd have been perfectly safe," Little Giant said. "You're a killer, a soldier of fortune. You scare us. Anyway, why not Mark? A gentleman, a Ph.D. . . ."

"Fired because of incompetence?" Mark asked. "Divorced because of dullness? Not trustworthy and inventive like you, dear brother."

"Ah . . ." Little Giant said. "Nah . . ."

"*You* always earned a living," Mathilde said. She kissed his ear. Syben tugged his beard. Mark ruffled his hair.

"Yeh," Little Giant said. "*Yeh.* Okay. Thanks." He tried to back off. Mathilde held on to his hand. "You were closest to your dad. He respected you, too."

"So when did *you* find out I was the thief?" Little Giant asked Mark.

Mark thought. "Oh . . . well, I suspected you from the start, of course, but I was sure when we landed in Hong Kong." He shook his head. "Tough bugger, aren't you? There we were, in shock, and you dared to bring it all up again." He imitated Little Giant's voice. "Who took the million, sister and brothers?"

"*Sister*," Mathilde said. "I like that." She patted Little Giant's hand.

"Why did you keep bringing it up?" Syben asked Little Giant. "Pride? Showing off?" He grinned. "Egocentricity again. True?"

"Man needs credits," Little Giant agreed.

"Modest again," Mathilde said. "In Hong Kong you tried to distract us." She gently tugged his hand. "You sweet little thing."

Mark laughed. "I heard what he did to you in the Tunisian swimming pool! Distracting! Hah."

Mathilde smiled.

Little Giant raised his left shoulder. "She enjoyed it, it seemed to me."

"Did you?" Mark asked Mathilde.

"It cured my itch," Mathilde said. "I had prickly heat. All that hot sun and sand."

"And when did *you* think you knew it was me?" Little Giant asked Syben.

"Let me see, now," Syben said. "I knew for sure when you messed with that camel. That was weird. You were weird, too—you have always been weird. And then I got thinking about Dad and the weirdly missing money, and how that must have been planned." Syben's perfect teeth showed in a strong, wide smile. "And I knew then that only you could have assisted him in that final twist, for all us others were far too normal."

Little Giant's eyes opened wide. "What's weird about throwing up on a camel?"

"Being that sick and still staying on a gigantic swaying camel is weird," Syben said. "I would have slipped off. You see things through."

"Nah . . ." Little Giant said softly.

"You're *such* a jolly good fellow," Mathilde sang.

"And so say all of us," Mark and Syben sang.

The waiter sang, too, for he hadn't yet been paid.